Happy Birthday
I Want A
Divorce

To: Rita

From: Kyle

"Don't be too shocked!"

Written By

Kyle Baker

[signature]

For information write:
Kyle Baker
kylebakerman@yahoo.com

Book cover design by: Greg Goodwin

Book design and layout by
Crystal Clear Publishing
Brandon, FL 33511

Printed in the United States of America

Library of Congress Catalog Card Number_____
ISBN 978-0692627631_____

TABLE OF CONTENTS

Dedication

I would like to dedicate this book to anyone who ever asks themselves the question "why me?" This book was written for those who may have experienced a true heartbreak and thought their world was coming to an end. It is for the woman that yearns for a loving man, yet his existence seems to lye only within a dream, and for the men whose only wish is to marry and live happily ever after with his chosen queen.

Acknowledgements

I would like to give all of the honor and glory to God. I know without him nothing is possible. I would like to thank him for giving me what I consider to be a gift in the form of writing along with the patience to do so.

The people that I would like to acknowledge deserve much more than just a simple thank you. I am forever indebted for all of your support throughout the journey of this book.

First, I would like to acknowledge my grandmother for everything she's ever taught me about life. Because of how she raised me, I learned to look at life's obstacles as prime opportunities which are specifically designed for one's advantage. This I believe applies to both male and female to achieve his or her purpose. I would like to thank my grandmother for everything she has ever done for me; even the rough love that she was never reluctant to give when I got out of line as a child. Whatever it took for her to raise me to be the man that I am now, I am forever grateful.

Bishop Samuel Wilson, thank you, sir for being one of the closest father figures in my life. Thank you for the countless phone calls of support during what I consider to be the lowest valley of my life.

Finally, to my brothers Keith Northcutt, Henry Mervin and Ray Daniels; the bond that I made with these gentlemen throughout this journey is one to cherish for a life time. One true friend on this earth is hard enough to find but I was fortunate enough to have crossed the paths of three. I can't begin to express my gratitude and genuine appreciation for your friendship.

Foreword

After meeting Mr. Kyle Baker some months ago, I realized I had met a young man who has had an abundance of life experience in his few years on this earth. "Happy Birthday, I Want A Divorce" weaves a tale of love, intrigue, hopelessness and faith.

Kyle threads the needle ever so slowly on a story that could have been life ending and changing but his main character is steadfast in the belief that the truth will conquer all evil thoughts and deeds.

Mr. Baker strolls down a lane of deceit, exhibitionist style addictions and anger to the degree of self-inflicted passion and pain. His writing is raw and is not for the faint at heart. Kyle uses descriptive words to make sure the reader knows the hurt and pain that can be felt when you decide that you would rather have death before dishonor.

I am thrilled to be a part of this young man's rise to author stardom and I look forward to enjoying future writings from such a talented man.

Donna M. Gray Banks
President, Ila's Diamonds LLC
Director of the F.R.E.S.H. Book
Festivals Author of Ila's Diamonds (a
trilogy)

Introduction

Why do bad things happen to good people in life? Is it pure circumstance, is it bad luck, or is it simply the will of God?

Sometimes I have wondered how people who do harm to others continue to live on this earth, be successful, and prosper, while nothing negative seems to happen to them at all. Despite the evil they have done to others, they are still "rising above the rest." God is, in fact, the last imaginable thought in their minds. Some people believe that they alone have placed themselves in situations that have led to their success with no help from God. Others understand that without Him nothing is possible and even though we are his children, sometimes in life we have to suffer.

Is this journey through life the test we must go through in order to inherit the Kingdom of Heaven? This is a question that is constantly argued over by those who study theology. If this in fact is the price that we have to pay to enter the Promise Land and all the wonderful things that are spoken of in the Bible, I think it is well worth the struggle. Having faith through some of the darkest situations of life is something that we as human beings must contend with. Why is that? I confess, for me personally, there was a time in my life when I had NO faith whatsoever.

That's when I think God decided to give me a wake-up call and show me who He really was. This is a story based on true events. I would like to take this time to say that I am **NOT** perfect. I don't consider myself to be "Holier than thou." Some of the things that you will read in this book may be offensive, but that does not mean that I don't believe in God or respect Him. I consider myself to be a **SERIOUS** work in progress. With that being said, if you don't think you can handle a book like this I **HIGHLY** suggest you put this one down and move on to something a little cushier. You've been warned!

Chapter 1- "My Georgia Peach"

I remember it just like it was yesterday. Around 11:59 PM one Friday night after leaving the airfield, I sat on my front porch, cracked open a cold beer and for the first time in my life, torched a stogie. This was my victory dance. I had just accomplished the most prestigious goal I had set in my life. About an hour prior to this moment I was officially signed off as a Blackhawk pilot. The dream that I'd been chasing for years was finally here, and I was living it. A few days later it was time to graduate. I remember standing there with pride in my dress blue uniform looking casket sharp with my classmates who all seemed to be very excited about this day. When the MC called my name I wanted to do a flip across the stage but decided to save myself the consequences that would surely follow.

Looking into the audience I could see my grandmother's eyes filled with tears, not tears of sadness, but tears of pride. My mother was murdered by her boyfriend when I was only five years old and I met my father for the first time at age 20. My grandmother stepped in with no hesitation to raise my sister and me. This graduation day was dedicated to her. She alone knew how hard I struggled to get into flight school. My mentor De'ray Campbell along with others was in attendance to see my big day. Lamar Pickens a childhood friend of mine, did the honors of pinning my aviation wings on my chest. This was by far one of the greatest days in my life.

A few days later, after spending the majority of the day sleeping, I finally woke up out of my state of rock star level drunkenness to a bowl of ramen noodles. There were two rogue chicken bones that had been severely butchered and somehow attached to an ATM receipt. Apparently I spent $260.00 at Teasers the local Tiki bar. "Damn it Glenn!" I berated myself. I decided to get up and try to do something fun for a change of pace. The fact was that the past year of flight school was dedicated to books, upon books, upon books. I've never had to read so much in my life! Anyway, I felt as if I deserved a little self-indulgence but living in Daleville Alabama it's a lost cause

for a guy like me. I mean let's face it, unless you like hunting,

dirt bikes, and girls with an odd number of teeth, the choices are

limited.

The reality of an unquenchable boredom quickly washed

over me. I was in Daleville. Even the name sounded

dull…Daleville, yuck! I ended up browsing through the many

"advertised lives" of my friends online. Just before logging off,

I noticed there was a column on the website labeled "*people you*

may know." I had never used this feature. I wasn't much of a

social media fan in the first place. Warily, I tried it out and sure

enough there were a few people I knew. One particular person I

knew struck my interest. Her name was Tammy Hill. The

reason Tammy was so intriguing to me was I previously had a

crush on her before I became a pilot. Just a few years earlier she

was a Buck Sergeant while I was a private first class. I was

sprung over this woman from the moment I saw her. Before my

balls dropped, I was always afraid to approach her because of her rank, not to mention the fact I didn't want to choke in the middle of a sentence. Well now the tables had turned and it was my well- earned chance to let her know how I had felt for so many years now. Here I was the one with the higher rank although in retrospect I don't believe it really mattered nevertheless, I was more confident. I sent a friend request along with a message attached that definitely explained my feelings. Now at the time I truly doubted that she would even returned my message. Gladly, I was wrong and to my surprise just a few hours later she sent a message back saying, "Hello Stranger, long time no see".

We immediately exchanged phone numbers and the conversation steadily escalated from there. It took a while but I finally came out verbally and told her how I felt. You would never guess what her response was. Ironically she told me she had been interested in me as well and that I should have approached her years ago. She then expressed that she thought I was with someone or married at the time. I chuckled a little bit and shook my head in disbelief. It was amazing to me that the woman I had a crush on for so many years was finally telling me that she felt the same way. We talked about hanging out sometime but I knew there was one "small" problem that stood in the way of us getting together. That problem was over 6000 miles away in a place that we Soldiers like to call the "sandbox," my problem had a name on it and that problem was still technically tied to me.

Her name was Gloria. Gloria was average height, Honduran and Nicaraguan mixed, had long jet black hair, and possessed an onion booty that would make any grown man cry. We had spent the past two years on and off with each other. Gloria was a good girl, she was a sweetheart, she was beautiful inside and out, but there were two major problems with Gloria that even the onion booty couldn't make okay. It seemed she loved drinking more than breathing air and there was also a slight issue with her legs staying closed when I wasn't around. When I first met Gloria she told me that every man she ever had in her life always dumped her after seeing how much of an alcoholic she was. Now like the good man that I am, I promised myself along with promising her, that I would be different from any other man. I would do any and everything that it took in order to tackle head on, any problems that came up. In hindsight I guess I thought I was a damn magician. The one thing that I didn't account for when I made that promise was the embarrassment that came along with her alcoholism. For example, she single-handedly ruined my 23rd and 24th birthdays. I bet you're wondering how that is possible. How can any person possibly destroy two birthdays back to back? Well with Gloria and tequila anything was possible!

On my 23rd birthday she took me out to a restaurant in Savannah, Georgia. The restaurant was pretty upscale and I must say I was impressed that she was doing this for me. It was a Japanese hibachi where they cooked the food in front of you on the grill. Due to the time of day, we had about an hour waiting period. Everything was going fine, things were cool, and the flirtation between us was setting the mood for a little extracurricular activity later on that night. After about 45 minutes while in the lobby waiting to be seated, I guess things were going a little too well, the calm before the storm was too good to be true because all of a sudden, Gloria got thirsty. Thirsty is the state of mind Gloria is in when nothing else but the bottle matters. She looked at me with those big brown eyes and the most pitiful face that she could put on. "Baby can I have a drink?" she asked.

I looked at her in disbelief but I tried my best not to let her know that she had just royally pissed me off. My initial thoughts were, "Not only is it my 23rd birthday but it is the first birthday I've had home from Iraq in the past two years." She also knew that I didn't believe in drinking and driving no matter how much or how little alcohol I had; which meant I'd end up driving. After a moment of split second thinking and not wanting to ruin the night I said "Sure, drink all you want Babe, I'll drive."

Little did I know but I'd just signed the permission slip

for a trip to and from hell. Gloria ordered one tall glass of Long Island ice tea. Most people that have had any real drinking experience in their life time will agree that long islands are pretty damn strong. I don't know the entire recipe but I know they consist of a mixture of many types of liquor including vodka, tequila, rum and gin. By the time we got seated Gloria's eyes were beginning to dance in her head like two loose marbles and her skin had developed the red tint it usually did when she drank. I would always jokingly refer to it as "the soul glow." As the night progressed the situation didn't get any better. We left the restaurant and instead of going home like I really wanted, we ended up going to a club in the downtown Savannah area, just alongside of River Street.

My optimism fooled me into believing that the rest of the night would end better than it had started. WRONG! As soon as we got into the club, Gloria darted to the bar like a bat out of hell with her ass on fire! She took down three shots of Patrón tequila and ordered **ANOTHER** Long Island ice tea! I sat in disbelief watching this chick drink for the next hour! To some relief, one of her co-workers was in the club with her boyfriend. We all managed to sit at the same table. The three of us shared the same embarrassment as our mutual friend harassed innocent passersby. By this time, she could barely keep her eyes open and her words were only annoying sounds that could be easily compared to a cat being strangled.

Another hour or so passed and she appeared to be coming to her senses a little more. Shortly there-after some guy asked if he could have a dance with her and without hesitation I said yes. I've always been pretty secure in all of my relationships and this guy made it sound as if the two of them were friends from work as well. THAT'S WHERE I SCREWED UP! They both went out to the dance floor and missed every opportunity to dance to the actual beat of the music. I remember thinking how funny it was to watch two drunken people try to dance. One had no idea what to do on the dance floor and the other suffered from a severe allergy to rhythm, plus she was white girl wasted. The two of them moved in a little closer; close enough to smell each other's hot drunk dragon breath. I paused for a moment to make sure I wasn't seeing things. Sure enough this was really happening. I quickly looked around my table to make sure I wasn't the only person seeing this and then I refocused my attention back to the dance floor. By the time I looked back in their direction Gloria and this guy were playing a rough game of tonsil hockey! The three of us stood up from the table almost at the same time all in shock at what we were seeing. I could feel the two of them looking at me expectantly and then back at Gloria on the dance floor. They stood out like a sore thumb in the midst of perhaps a few hundred people.

My initial thought was to go over and crack the guy in the face with the empty beer bottle that was left on our table. I think God was with me at that very moment for sure. I took a deep breath and walked over to them as calmly as I could. My palms began to sweat, I couldn't stop grinding my teeth, and there was a trickle of perspiration running down the right side of my face. I could feel my heart pounding on the inside of my chest. My pulse was probably off the charts. By the time I got there they had stopped kissing. I grabbed her by the hand and told him that we had to go to which he seemed upset about. I gave him one more look that pretty much expressed the rage I had inside. He smartly backed away with both hands in the air.

The funny thing about this entire situation, besides the fact that I didn't react like a normal guy would, was the fact that I was able to slip off the $3,000.00 engagement ring that I had given her just a few months prior to this "birthday celebration". She never even noticed! Just when I didn't think things could possibly get any worse they did. We were on our way to my car with me basically dragging her over my shoulder down the sidewalk when she suddenly collapsed in the middle of the street. There I was, on River Street, one of the most popular tourist locations in the state of Georgia and my fiancé was passed out while dozens of people stopped to watch the show. Soon the cops showed up and asked me if she was ok. Sarcastically, I told the black officer that she was "narcoleptic and trying to take a nap." To my surprise, he laughed. He told me to take the knuckles of my fist and rub them firmly up and down her sternum. I wasn't sure what that was supposed to do but I did as I was told and without delay she woke up.

The two officers watched her long enough for me to get my car. They told me to park on the wrong side of the street just to load her into the vehicle. When I got out of the car, another officer pulled up with his blue lights on and blocked traffic on both sides. They all assisted with getting her in the car, told me goodnight and wished me luck as they could all see my frustration. I was grateful that the cops weren't jerks about the entire situation. I couldn't believe this was happening on my birthday of all days. Getting home as soon as possible was my number one priority. It felt like the thirty-minute drive back to Fort Stewart was a two-day journey. We were only half way home when Gloria woke up for the third time out of her drunken nap, but this time she was dry heaving. I screamed at her to warn me if she was going to throw up but before I could even finish, she shot vomit like a rocket propelled grenade all over my windshield. I felt my stomach start to rumble as if someone was churning butter. The stench of rotten food mixed with liquor filled the air in my car. Gloria's vomit smelled like an animal had crawled inside of her belly and died. Finally we arrived to the parking lot of my apartment.

Despite the fact that I was hot as a pistol and still in a state of disbelief about everything that had happened that night, I still had the decency to take care of this girl. I kept thinking to myself that if I was the average man I would have definitely left her at the club in Savannah. If I had done that however, more than likely something bad would have happened to her and God knows I wouldn't have been able to live with myself after that. I carried her inside of my apartment and straight to the bathroom. I ran some water hoping that a warm bath would help ease her state of mind, but somehow it only made things worst. Gloria was like a cat in water, not happy at all. She suddenly slapped me in the face and told me that I was an evil person. To this day her bipolar tendencies confound me when she drinks. After taking a few hits to the face I gave up on the rest of the bath and washed the remaining vomit out of her hair. I wrapped her head up in a towel and laid her down in my bed. I spent the night of my 23rd birthday on a blow up mattress.

The very next day was Mother's Day. I was asked to play the drums for one of the local churches in a town called Allenhurst which is about 15 minutes away from my apartment. When I got up to get ready Gloria was still passed out sleep. I checked to make sure she had a pulse. Thankful she hadn't died in the middle of the night from alcohol poisoning, I took a long shower to help with the sleepiness, got dressed and got on the road. At church the service was everything that I thought it would be. It was very uplifting and it helped to ease my mind. The band played a few songs and then it was time for the speaker. Given that it was Mother's Day the preacher began his message by addressing all of the mothers, wives, and soon to be wives sitting in the congregation. After acknowledging all of the women in the church he brought things to order by opening his message with the words "A Good Woman."

The things he said in reference to what a good woman was and the qualities that she should have as a good woman; was the complete opposite of Gloria. Tears started to build up in my eyes like small buckets of water. I could feel myself breaking down and was almost on the brink of no return. I quickly managed to control the bad plumbing and left the church with one resolution on my mind…Gloria had to go! I drove slowly back to the apartment taking all the time I could to gather my thoughts. "It's time for a change" I encouraged myself as I pulled up to the apartment complex. At this point in my life I had never broken up with anybody. Being the dumpee was my usual role but never the dumper. The anxiety began to build and I had no clue what I was about to do or say for that matter. I walked in the bedroom only to see Gloria's mouth gaping wide open as if she was catching raindrops. My devious side told me to pour a few shots of hot sauce in her mouth but I quickly changed my mind after remembering this was no laughing matter. I grabbed a few plastic bags and began packing her things as fast as I could. She woke up from the noise of the bags and me purposely slamming the dresser drawers closed. "Good morning baby," she said sleepily. I blatantly ignored her while heading to the kitchen to get another bag. When I came back in the room it was obvious that she could sense something was wrong. She reached for her glasses on the night stand and took a moment to gather herself before making another attempt to speak to me. This time she had a bit of sarcasm in her voice which would be the spark I needed to unleash the rage that had been inside of me. "You really did a number on me last night!" I shouted at the top of my lungs and I think it scared me more than her because I'd never raised my voice at her before. Her posture changed almost instantly as she sat straight up in the bed. I could see the look of fear cross her face but could care less about how she felt. I wanted her to hurt the way she hurt me.

"What are you talking about?" she asked. It infuriated me that she couldn't remember the events from the previous night or at least she continued to claim she had no recollection of them.

I've always believed people are conscious of their actions when they drink but blame it on the alcohol the next day because of regret. She normally suffered from short term amnesia on a day to day basis and I would always take advantage of her lack of memory under normal circumstances. This however, was one time I wish she could recall what happened. "What do you remember Gloria," I asked. She swallowed hard and tried to think of the past night even harder.

"I remember being in the club with you, we were dancing and having a good time" she replied. "You know that's awfully funny because we didn't dance one time together last night" I said. "Here's what really happened. "First you asked me if you could have a drink at the restaurant, which I thought was very selfish considering the fact that it was my birthday and you know how I feel about drinking and driving." "Honey I'm so sorry" she began. "Oh but wait there's more so don't say a damn word until I'm done talking!" "After dinner, even though I didn't want to, we went to the club anyway."

"I just knew you couldn't mess up the rest of the night, but I was wrong about that too. As soon as we got in the club you acted like Patrón was running out of style. I'm sure you spent all your money within the first thirty minutes on drinks. Sergeant De la Cruz and her boyfriend can back me up on the way you carried on the entire time. At this point I was so disgusted I didn't even want to be around you. Just when I thought things couldn't get any worse you ended up making out with some guy on the dance floor." "Oh my God! Glenn, are you serious?" she uttered in a state of shock. "Why would I lie about something like that Gloria?" "Please forgive me baby" she mumbled with a soft ragged voice. Her eyes filled with tears and disbelief as I went on with the story. I continued to pack her things while giving her all the remaining details from my "birthday celebration." When I finished loading her bags up by the door, I changed my clothes and walked out. I paused just before getting in my car and realized that there was still vomit on the inside of my windshield. I opened the passenger door to see a large trail of rotten food particles that lead to the center console. "How could a woman so beautiful be so disgusting at the same time" I thought. I sat on the hood of my car for a moment to cool off. Seeing the vomit vividly reminded me of everything that happened. While in my own thoughts, my phone loudly went off. I swiped my finger across the screen and there was a message was from her. "Baby I am so sorry for ruining your birthday, I don't know what was going through my head. Please forgive me and I will do whatever it takes to fix this" it read.

As expected the very apologetic text messages flowed in like clockwork. Little did she know but I was serious about my decision this time. I replied back "*leave my key on the kitchen counter on your way out*". There was a long pause between the messages and then; "Baby, where is my ring?" she asked. She finally noticed that there was a fairly nice size of hardware missing from her finger. "Gloria you lost your ring at the club" I said. Technically this wasn't a lie but it was definitely a shade of the truth. She called me frantically screaming "Please tell me that's not true Glenn!" "Listen, that's the last thing on my mind right now, you proved to me that you don't deserve a ring anyway," I said. "I feel like a jackass for even buying you that damn ring," I told her. We went on lashing at each other for another hour or so until I just had enough.

A few months passed while I started my career as a flight school student before Gloria and I eventually talked again. Occasionally she would text me asking to go to dinner or something like that but I would make up excuses or just ignore her completely. I guess her persistence wore me down after months of text messages, phone calls, and apology emails. We planned a dinner date at Olive Garden on a Saturday night. I was hesitant about meeting her in the beginning because bad memories of my birthday kept flashing through my mind. I managed to suppress my thoughts when I arrived at the parking lot of the restaurant. I walked in the door and was greeted by the hostess.

"Good evening sir and welcome to Olive Garden," she said. "Do you have a reservation?" I paused to answer as I glanced around the tables in the room only to see Gloria waving her hand in the air. "My party is already here," I said while pointing towards her. The hostess walked me to the table; Gloria stood up and greeted me with a hug and a small kiss to the cheek. The conversation between the two of us was slow but gradually built as time passed. I think we both tried to avoid the birthday incident and to be honest it was pleasing to do so. We actually laughed and had a good time. This was the first time in a long time that we enjoyed each other's company. After dinner we decided to continue the date with a movie. I can't remember the name of the film but I do remember me and her sitting in the back of the movie theater. There were only a few people in the theater with us and they were all pretty spread out across the seats.

She made it a point to raise the center arm rest before we sat down just so she could be closer to me. I already knew what this would eventually lead to but for whatever reason I decided to go along with it. About twenty minutes into the movie she slid her hand from my knee up to my gun holster. After slowly caressing the hard case, she "unzipped" the safety on my pistol. Locked and loaded I began to blow her brains out for the next thirty minutes. Before she could swallow my bullets we left the movie theater. Given the circumstances it would have been pretty intense to seize the moment, but Gloria usually screamed when she rode my roller coaster.

We raced to my place to finish what we started in the back of the movie theater. We undressed as if our clothes were on fire! Never making it to the bed, I bent her over the sink and began to deliver the package she had just ordered express. I wrapped a fist full of her long black hair around my hand and curled my arm as if I was in the gym. The point of my elbow rested perfectly in the center of her back. Gloria was well over due for a thorough spinal tap and I was obliged to assist her with her check-up. As I sent shock waves through her body and probably her soul, she began to utter in Spanish. I for one couldn't understand a damn word of it but I can only imagine the things she was saying. I breathed quickly as "round one" came to a hot and sweaty end. The night ended well and you would think this would be the beginning of a better future between the two of us. This was true for a while until it was time for Gloria's first deployment in the Army.

Now I won't bad mouth all women in the military, but I will say that 95% of them develop very promiscuous sexual habits when they're deployed. The usual and more common excuses are, "I got so lonely," or "I had a vulnerable moment (4 times)," or my all-time favorite excuse "I thought you were doing the same thing." I know what you're thinking, men are no different, we aren't; but be reminded that people are people. Even with me warning Gloria about the type of environment she would be faced with, the number of men and women who would try to get in her pants, plus the overall persistence of vultures she probably worked with on a day to day basis, nothing could prepare me for what was to come.

May 10th 2010, my phone rings at 9:35 in the morning. I sat up in bed, wiped the sleep from the crack of my eyes and said "Hello." Gloria's voice surprised me because this was the first time she'd ever called this early. What was more alarming was the fact that she was crying. Her voice crackled with each attempt to tell me something, but I couldn't understand exactly what it was. Finally, she composed herself and said, "I have to tell you something and it's very hard for me." "Go ahead" I replied. It was almost as if I knew already what she was about to say.

Sure as hell she paused, took a deep breath and then "Glenn I can't continue to live this lie, I've been cheating on you for the past four months." Now there was a lot I wanted to say

and definitely more I could have said. Ironically, I giggled and

couldn't stop giggling. Obviously puzzled as to why I was

laughing, Gloria asked what was so funny. "Not only did you

destroy my 23rd birthday, you kissed another man in the club in

front of me. Then to top that you lost your engagement ring,

which I have by the way, now you're telling me that you couldn't

keep your legs closed for a few months? Gloria have a nice life!"

"Glenn please, listen to me," she begged. "I had a weak moment."

Before she could even get another word out I interrupted, "Gloria

kick rocks with open toe shoes on and don't ever call me again!"

Chapter 2- "I'm Not On That Level"

In the end Gloria was everything that a man didn't want; a lush and a slut. But with her being a thing of the past I could now finally look towards my future, my future with Tammy. After reuniting with my dream lover our relationship escalated fast, like a shell from a gun to be exact. I thought that Gloria was the worst thing that could have ever happen to me. So after finally having Tammy in my life, I wasted no time going down on one knee.

When Lamar heard the news that I was getting married to Tammy, I think he reacted like any other friend would have, especially since he was someone who has had serious female issues in the past. Lamar had been married twice before. He was the father of six kids from five different women, and let's not mention the $4,000.00 a month in child support he had to dish out. This probably was enough to convince any man to run for the hills but not me. I was head over heels in love with Tammy and nothing could stop me from having her as my wife.

The love that I felt for this woman was a love that I couldn't risk losing at all. I flew to Alabama and we were married shortly thereafter.

This was by far the happiest day of my life, and I was proud to tell anyone I was a married man.

Later on that night the chariot dropped us off at the hotel suite that I reserved weeks prior to the wedding day. Little did she know but the entire staff helped me to plan the perfect night. There was a blindfold left on the handle of the door that I used to cover her eyes. I led her into the room by the clutch of her hand. As she walked the scent of chocolate and her favorite perfume lingered in the air. I gently slid off the blind fold, to reveal the rose petals that covered the floor and trailed to the Jacuzzi hot tub filled with bubbles. The lights were dimmed and small candles flickered throughout the room. Music played softly in the background as I poured a glass of champagne. She pulled me in closer to her body; so close I could feel the rhythm of her heart beating against my chest. I gazed into her eyes which spoke silent words of sexual desire and with no hesitation we melted together with a kiss. The soft touch of her lips made my pulse race and my skin began to tingle.

Before I knew it I heard the sound of buttons being ripped from my shirt. We fell into a pile of roses that were scattered on the bed. The two of us raced down to our birthday suits which was the perfect attire throughout the night until the brink of dawn. I was her dark knight and she was my Nubian queen. She began to polish my sword as I caressed the center of her throne with the tip of my tongue. I divided her smooth legs of caramel, and with each stroke of passion I could feel the pit of her valley. Her nails dug deeper into my back with each thrust of my lower half. I glanced up towards the ceiling and caught a glimpse of her toes which were locked in a curled position. Motivated by the moans coming from her throat, the steady rocking of the headboard and the sight of her gripping the sheets, we consummated our vows until sunrise. It was a night to remember and one could only imagine many nights like this to come in the future.

The time we had together as newlyweds was short lived due to me having to depart on official orders to South Korea. I wasn't thrilled at all for the move because I heard nothing but horror stories about the lifestyle for Soldiers serving there. The one and only positive thing that I was looking forward to was being reunited with my beautiful bride and new daughter in a few short months. Tammy would be following me after she completed her tour as an Army recruiter. It is amazing how plans suddenly turn for the worst in the military. One day after a few hours of flying, I received an email from Tammy saying that we needed to talk. I called home immediately out of fear that something terrible had happened. "What's up?" I asked eagerly.

"Listen, I was contacted by my branch manager yesterday stating that I will no longer be going to Korea. We spent the last thirty minutes on the phone this morning discussing other possibilities but Korea is not an option," she said. "Why?" I asked, frustrated and confused. "He said that since I've been stateside for so long as a recruiter, I needed to be assigned to a unit that would be deploying to Iraq soon." "I don't understand, you have already been to Iraq three times and did you mention the fact that you have a husband in Korea?" "Yes said Tammy, he told me that was not a concern of his nor the Army's. The only choices that I have are Fort Hood or Fort Knox. He told me that I could pick or he would pick for me. They're going to work on a follow on assignment for you after you leave Korea." Yeah right, I thought to myself. Tammy paused… "So where do you want to go?" she asked. "Well with me being a pilot the only place that I can go is Fort Hood, so I guess that's our next home." "Listen, she said with a sharp voice, I don't need you trying to do anything about this behind my back, just let it go. I don't think Fort Hood is going to be that bad. My best friend Kelly is there, I have some family in the area, and Ashley can finally have a relationship with her father because he's there too." I agreed, but after I got off the phone I felt uneasy, like I had been played. Let's be real, she was pretty excited about going to Texas. For some reason something just didn't feel right and I wanted to make sure my gut wasn't steering me wrong. I scheduled a meeting with my commander Major Zackary later on that week. When we sat down in his office he could clearly see the concern on my face so he immediately asked what was wrong. "Sir I'm new to this side of the Army with me being an officer now. I just want to make sure things are in order with something concerning my marriage." "Ok well spill it Glenn, tell me what seems to be the problem," he asked. "Sir I don't want to take up too much of your time, so I'll get straight to the point. My wife was supposed to be coming to Korea as you already know, but now her branch manager is telling her that Korea is not an option. He said that she needs to go to a unit that is going to deploy soon.

I just don't understand why they would do this especially considering the fact that she didn't volunteer to be a recruiter. The Army placed her in that position and now we're being punished for it because she hasn't deployed in the last three years. How is this fair or even right? Tell me if I'm out of my lane here," I begged. "Well Glenn I think as Soldiers we are sometimes asked to sacrifice more than we signed up for. If I were in your shoes, I would have the same concerns." "So where do we go from here sir?" "I'll make some calls, said Major Zackary. I can't promise you anything but I will try to squash this crap before it gets out of hand." Well a few weeks passed and nothing good came from my efforts, it ended up becoming a train wreck and things actually got worse.

I got a text from Tammy that was very disturbing and it would only be the tip of the iceberg as the destruction unfolded.

"I got an email today saying that my school date for the Senior Leaders Course was cancelled. Now I have to report to Fort Hood even earlier than I'm supposed to. I will be deploying to Iraq within fifteen days of me getting there. Glenn I hope you're happy now because I told you to leave this alone!"
Wifey

This didn't make me happy at all, why would I be? I remember thinking to myself, this is clear retribution that someone is taking against my family but I didn't know why. I was simply trying to keep my family together. "Who did I piss off," I thought out loud. I was in the dog house for a few days or so but we eventually talked about the situation and resolved our problems. Little did I know, but the problems were only going to get worse. A month later, Tammy asked me to come home early so we could see each other before she deployed.

The time we would spend separated would be about a year to a year and a half, so seeing each other one last time seemed like the smart thing to do. I booked a flight and arrived in Mobile a few weeks later. When I got to the airport there were other families greeting their love ones, friends hugging each other, and couples kissing for the first time in what appeared to be quite a while. Tammy was nowhere to be found. About an hour later she finally showed up dressed in a pair of sweats and garnished with pink hair rollers. "Sorry I'm late," she whispered. I had some other things I had to take care of." I leaned in for a hug and kiss, but got the affection of a friend, definitely not a lover. I stored the moment in the back of my head, but I must say the suspense was beginning to creep into my mind. Later on that night after being away from my wife for four months, I was sure the sheets would be on fire between the two of us. Boy was I wrong! With every attempt to kiss her, or even touch her for that matter, my hands were slapped and I was being pushed away. For a moment I thought she was role playing because that was something we had previously discussed but then I suddenly sensed that she was serious! "Baby what's wrong?" I asked.

"Listen Glenn, I've got a lot on my mind she said and I need some time to get back on that level." Confused by the entire situation, I chose to sleep on the couch and tried to figure out what "level" she was referring to. Days passed with nothing between the two of us that would signify newlyweds. I couldn't even pinch her if I wanted to. "What is going on" I kept thinking. A normal couple would have been all over each other. By the end of the week I was even more concerned with this "level" thing she had previously spoke of; so I asked the question that I think any man would have asked. "Who is he and how long have you guys been seeing each other?" "Glenn there is no one else, like I told you before I just have a lot on my mind." "Well what is it about me that you obviously have a problem with considering that fact that you won't even touch me," I asked. "I don't know I just really feel like we rushed this marriage. I think that we should have waited a little longer." "I understand that entirely I said, but what's done is done now, we can't go back in time and undo the past. Do you still love me at least?" Tammy gazed down towards her ring finger as if she was contemplating her answer. Her hesitation was killing me but soon the inevitable truth was spoken… "Glenn I love you, but I'm not in love with you anymore. I don't know how to say this so I'm just going to come out and say it… I want a divorce." This was the first blow to the chest I took from Tammy and I think it surprised me more than anything. I left the house to avoid the confrontation. There was a Mexican restaurant about a mile or so away from her apartment so I headed that way.

I hopped in my jeep and sped off in a furious rage. I ran every light without a single cop pulling me over. The restaurant was packed and the hostess informed me that it would be a one hour wait before I could be seated. I left the parking lot headed to the interstate. Driving on the expressway has always seemed to calm me down in a strange way. I was finally cooling off and then my phone rang. Glancing at the caller ID, I could faintly see Tammy's name flash across the screen. Curious as to what she would say, I answered. "Listen I just called you to tell you that I'm really sorry all of this happened, but I can't continue to live a lie. I don't love you anymore and getting married was the worst mistake I've made in my life." I ended the call with the swipe of my finger, but in my mind Tammy's voice still lingered. I could feel my body tremble with each mile that passed, I glanced down at the speedometer only to see that I was driving too fast. The jeep was driving itself in what appeared to be the blink of an eye. I was headed straight towards a telephone pole but couldn't stop. I finally gained control of the car but it was too late. I collided with the pole. The angle of impact caused the car to roll down the side of a small cliff about four or five times. I felt like I was inside of a dryer as I tumbled to a halt. Gathering my thoughts, I managed to stumble out of the jeep and into a patch of flowers alongside the highway. A few minutes later there was a voice of an older lady ringing in my ears as if she was calling me from the end of a long hallway. The next thing I remember was being placed on a stretcher and then into the back of an ambulance. The lady in the back tried to ask me questions but I couldn't form the words for what I wanted to say. My body wasn't in any pain at all but for some reason I just couldn't talk. By the time we got to the hospital the police informed me they had contacted my wife and that's when I began to cry. The nurse in the room was in the middle of adjusting my I.V. cable. Genuinely concerned, she asked me what was wrong. I briefly explained the situation but quickly ended it to avoid the mental pain again. A few minutes later Tammy's commander showed up to the hospital. He told me that Tammy would not be coming because she said Ashley had school in the morning. "I'm glad she can't be here" I remember thinking. After a few hours of lying there, I was finally released to his care.

Fortunately for me I only suffered a minor bruise to the back of my head from the accident. He drove me back to Tammy's apartment which was the last place I wanted to go. I knocked on the door and she answered almost immediately. With no hesitation the first words out of her mouth were "Glenn did you do that on purpose?" I stood there in place trying to make sure I understood what she said. "So you're asking if I ran my jeep into a pole and down the side of a cliff on purpose. Good night Tammy, I'll be out of here in the morning." She crossed her arms and walked back down the hallway to her bed room.

May 10th 2011, happy 25th to me! Being in an unfamiliar city and not knowing anyone besides her, Tammy was the only person I had to take me to the wrecker's lot. My entire luggage was still in the back of the car along with other important documents. To add to the list of problems the owner of the lot charged $100.00 a day for storage of wrecked vehicles. There was silence for the first twenty minutes of the trip and then she spoke. "Do you understand why I don't want to be married anymore," she asked. "Yes but no. Yes, because you are upset right now, but no because we haven't even tried at this marriage. Four months is not enough time to really be married. You are the love of my life baby." "Please don't call me baby!" she screamed. "I don't want you in my life, whenever things don't go your way it's a problem and I'm not going to put up with it!" I could feel the temperature of my body heating up but yet my mind couldn't help but wonder what is it about me my birthday and women? Somehow the celebration of birth was always followed by the proverbial kiss of death.

I wanted to strangle her with the same seatbelt she was wearing. Traffic was bumper to bumper and slow enough that I decided to jump out and finish the trip on foot. People blew their horns at me as I cut through traffic to get to the other side of the road. I could hear footsteps running up behind me as I walked down the side of the pavement. Tammy's voice blared over all the car horns around me. "Glenn! Stop please!" she begged. Tammy had driven up close enough to catch me. "Please talk to me." "For what, what the hell do we have to talk about?" This woman must be bipolar I thought to myself. One minute she's the devil's advocate and the next she's begging to talk to me...

Chapter 3-"911 what's your emergency?"

"Why won't you just talk to me, please Glenn I'm right here just calm down." "Tammy there's nothing else left to say," I explained. "You said it all a few minutes ago, remember? Just know I would have never done this to you and especially not on your damn birthday! How could you?" "Riddle me this I asked, why did you marry me in the first place? You knew from day one you didn't want this. How long have you been thinking about calling it quits? We've been married for four months and you want to give up? That's a celebrity marriage record. Is it because I tried to fight to have you and Ashley in Korea with me?" My mind raced with countless questions.

Tammy's voice crackled with each word while she struggled to fight back tears. I was 38 hot, cocked like a pistol, and couldn't really understand why she was crying at all. I mean hell; I wasn't the one who just dropped a bomb on someone's nut sack! "Just stay away from me, you've done enough," I said. I started walking down the highway towards a town called

Greenville which was 165 miles away. To this day I'm not sure what my plan was to get there, but I was determined to do it. I was about a mile or so up the road when a highway patrolman pulled up behind me in his car. I could hear his tires cracking over the pebbles on the road. He was so close to me, I could feel the heat from the hood of his car. "What a prick," I thought to myself. "Sir stop walking; let's not make a scene here on the side of the road ok?" I remember thinking to myself, "did he really need to use a megaphone to tell me that" but I did as I was told. The driver along with his partner approached me casually. I guess they could see I wasn't a threat to anyone besides myself or at least that's what they believed according to her. "Hey man what's your name?" The patrolman was average height, had a bit of a pot belly, and he spoke with a heavy southern accent. I could tell he himself was probably born and raised in Alabama. "My name is Glenn."

"Hi Glenn, my name is Officer Ivan B. Stone and this Here is my partner, Officer Benedict Daley." So, you want to tell us why you're walking down the highway, I mean it's 104 degrees on the heat index today and as you can see traffic is pretty thick?" "Sir, bums walk up and down the highway every day and you guys don't bother them why are you bothering me?" "Well Glenn that's a true statement, and the only reason we're stopping you is because a young lady called 911 and reported a possible suicidal man walking down the highway." He looked down at his notepad and asked; "are you married to a Tammy Taylor?" "Well, I am for the moment I said, but she just asked for a divorce. It's only been four months but I'm currently serving in Korea. Typical Army marriage you know, I'm sure someone's been knocking her down while I've been gone. It happens all the time."

"Well Glenn that's awful and I'm so sorry to hear that, but I can't have you walking down the highway where they're innocent people driving by." I bit my tongue but couldn't hold back. "Once again sir, what's wrong with me minding my own business, not bothering a damn soul and simply taking a stroll down this highway?" "That's just it Glenn, she's saying you're suicidal, and I can't risk putting other lives in danger you know what I mean?" His southern drawl annoyed me with each word that he spoke.

"That's her word against mine but I can assure you she's a habitual liar, she lies to her own mother like it's nobody's business and for no reason!" "Yeah that's true as well Glenn, it is your word against hers, but let's be frank man, where are you headed?" "I'm going to get my luggage in Greenville." "They both giggled a bit and shook their heads in disbelief. "Do you realize that's 165 miles away son?" I paused for a moment and did my best to hide the embarrassment. It's frustrating how dumb I can be when I'm upset about something. I didn't have a comeback and this pissed me off even more. He just boxed me into this verbal corner and I was usually pretty good at talking myself out of a sticky situation. "Look sir she just broke my heart alright? I've never been hurt so badly before in my life and didn't know the reason why, especially when I've done nothing to deserve this. I seem to pick the wrong women all the damn time. Not that it's your problem, but my ex was a raging alcohol and now this? I can't win for losing." "I understand that Glenn, it's happened to all of us, buddy I'll tell you what, I've been married five times in my 44 years of living. Now I won't say I was the perfect husband all the time but sometimes things happen that we can't control. I walked in on my first wife and my best friend doing some other than Godly things. My second wife left me because she said I didn't make enough money, well I'm rambling now Glenn. My point is women can be cruel but man this is not the way to handle it." I leaned up against the guardrail and closed my eyes. The sound of cars passing by was steadier now as traffic slowly began to pick up. I still couldn't believe this was happening. "Now listen man, I'm going to give you three choices. You can go back with your wife and try to work this out, I can take you in and hold you at the jail house until someone comes to get you, or you go to the hospital and let them check you out to make sure you're ok." "Well, I'll tell you right now sir option one and two are off the table. She doesn't want me there and I don't want to be around her. There's a good chance we might see black dresses and hear some slow singing if we're near each other, know what I mean?" "Was that a threat to Tammy," he asked. I deflected his question with a distracting response, she's trying her best to hurt me; those are crocodile tears running down her cheeks, and me going to jail for nothing is crazy! How long would I be in the hospital?" "They'll hold you for a few hours to make sure everything is ok and then they'll let you go." "That's it I asked?" "That's it Glenn, I promise." Part of the reason I despise most cops now is because they lie so badly. When I checked into the hospital they immediately strapped me down to a table, I was restrained by my wrists and ankles. I was then taken to the fifth floor of the hospital. This was the psychiatric ward, how the hell I ended up there is beyond me. I kept thinking to myself, "That cop really got over on me." I had no clue things would go down like this after flying 14 hours home from Korea. I felt like I was in a horror movie about to be gutted like a fish and hung from chains dangling from the ceiling. This was the birthday from Hell! Not only has my wife told me the worst news a man can hear, but now I was in the nut house mixed in with real psychos. They took me to a room that had windows with a screen surface and reinforced steel bars attached. There wasn't a single power outlet on the walls, no TV, no radio, and the shower head was a modified hole in the ceiling with weak pressure. Even the toilet and sink were enclosed together, made of hard plastic. The nurse would come in the room every thirty minutes to check on me. Other than that she would attempt to feed me antidepressants which I fed to a hole in the side of my mattress. Tammy was on anti-depressants and I for one didn't want to end up twisted in the head like she was.

Chapter 4-"You Don't Need to Know"

While standing there in formation, I started to replay the vacation from hell over and over again in my mind. My chain of thought was abruptly interrupted by the sound of Reveille blaring over the speakers. After we saluted the flag, the first sergeant's voice echoed across the field as he led the company through warm up drills for PT. It actually felt good to work out. It was a warm, June morning, and the weather was probably about 90% humidity, causing most of us to sweat, but the sweat was a good sweat. In a very strange way it was almost soothing to the soul, maybe even therapeutic now that I think about it.

We worked out for an hour or so and then he released us for a 09:00 work call. Major Zackary briefed the company on the tasks that had to be accomplished that day, after which we all walked to our cars. Just before I could reach the handle of mine, Major Z called my name. "Glenn I need to speak to you." I turned around quickly only to notice Major Z with his arms crossed in front of his chest. "Yes sir?" "So how was your leave?" he asked. I had debated how I would answer this question the entire flight back to Korea. Up until this point I had so many different scenarios that I'd contemplated using and just when I needed at least one of them nothing was coming to mind; I just blanked out.

Being creative enough to tell the truth without giving all the details was mentally exhausting, not to add to the fact that Major Zackary was a well-known poker player who could probably call my bluff with very little effort. "Sir my leave was fine, I replied." "C'mon Glenn don't try to pull the blinds over my eyes because that's not what I heard." "I have my sources that tell me differently," he continued. "Ok sir, well to be honest the entire vacation was terrible." "My wife asked for a divorce and I still don't know why," I explained. "My reaction wasn't the best, but since then I have gotten counseling and other methods of help to include guidance from my pastor. Sir I'm good to go now and I'm focused on moving forward with the rest of my life."

I tried my best to sell myself to probably the most stubborn customer ever. He just wasn't buying it. "Well Glenn the news I got was a little more disturbing, something about some suicidal ideations. So with that being said, I'm ordering you to go see a Chaplin or make an appointment to behavioral health, the choice is yours." "Roger that Sir will do." I knew instantly which route I would take. Speaking to a Chaplain would almost be like an interview, as long as I said the right lines I would get the job.

This was true in my opinion for most Chaplains in the Army, there's a formality most of them follow. It was always cut, dry, and straight to the point. Also nothing would be documented if I stayed within my left and right limits. If I chose the other side of the coin however, by going to behavioral health, things would be a little different. It automatically gets documented in your medical records and who knows what affect that could have had on my aviation career. Bottom line there was no way I was going to see an Army shrink. You take a chance by reporting headaches and even back pains in aviation, let alone going to mental health. That was the quickest way to be grounded from flight status and I knew it.

The Chaplain's visit was just like I had envisioned it would be. "Mr. Taylor how are you doing this morning," the older gentlemen politely asked. "I have a pulse sir, as best I can for the moment." "I understand that chief." "Well what brings you by my office this morning young man?" "Well sir, I was actually ordered to come see you following some incidents that took place while I was home on leave." "Ooh," he gasped, as if he was shocked to hear that something bad had happened to me. It was like he was already "my friend" of many years. "Well let me ask you this first; are you suicidal?" "Not at all sir, extremely crushed by the news, but definitely not suicidal. Surprised that he would ask that question even before hearing the story, I played off my facial expressions. "Ok are you homicidal?"

"Not at all sir," I said. "Please forgive me," he added, but I have to ask those questions, you know how protocol goes right?" "I understand sir, no worries." "So, Chief Taylor, tell me about the events that took place while you were home." I paused for a moment and stared into his grey eyes, examining them for any clues that would reveal someone un-trust worthy. He cracked a slight smile as if he knew exactly what I was doing. Then again maybe the old man was actually genuine, I couldn't tell. I began my story with a bit of a giggle. "Sir I had the worst time of my life and I'm laughing at the fact of how jacked up it actually was. It was almost surreal. Those thirty days seemed like something out of a movie to be honest with you."

I told him the entire story in about an hour or so. "Glenn that's horrible, sorry you had to experience that tragedy, but you know," my eyes followed his hand as he reached for his coffee. He cleared his throat and sipped from the steaming hot cup. It always puzzled me how some people could drink coffee in 100-degree weather. He carefully placed his mug back on the desk. "Sometimes in life Glenn, bad things happen to good people. I guarantee you though; you will rise from this pit of sorrow." I'm sure that line was straight out of the manual, like something they taught him to say at the school of Chaplain's, but it sounded good, at least for the moment. "Well Glenn, what do you want from me, how can I help you?"

I ended the conversation just as quickly as I could. "Sir, I was just told to come see you by my commander. I guess he wants to make sure I'm ok given your feedback of course; how do you feel about me sir?" I was courteous enough to make it seem as if his input was any concern of mine. Clearly knowing that the entire conversation would have to stay confidential, I felt better about approaching my commander later on that day. Not that I planned on deceiving him in anyway, but the details of the conversation only existed between Chaplin Swinton and myself. Throughout the conversation with the Chaplin I stayed well within my limits. I never mentioned anything about killing myself or others for that matter such as Tammy, and I didn't break down into tears. "Well Glenn, I certainly think you have had a hardship, but you seemed to be handling it well. I feel with time just like with anything else in life, you will put this behind you. You seemed to be a very bright young man, and I know you will find your way through this storm." More of those lines from schoolhouse," I thought. Enough with the pity party it was time to go. "Thank you sir for your time, I'm sure Major Zackary will be giving you a call, or perhaps you can call him to let him know how well our meeting went." I stood up and exhaled in relief that this was over. I shot my palm out like a true politician, gave him the old hand to shoulder pat, and walked out the door. I reported back to Major Z that I had met with the Chaplin, and that he would be contacting him soon.

Weeks passed by and I hadn't heard anything at all from Tammy. My guidance from Bishop Williams, my pastor was to ignore all emails, phone calls etc. until she spoke to me better. The emails in the past were nothing short of Satan burning them in stone himself. I truly believe he, "the devil," may have proof read a few of her emails, made corrections with blood, and gave advice on how they could be more ruthless. I say this because the letters she wrote me were beyond evil and were more demonic than anything.

The end of the month was approaching; I was tired of being depressed and needed to get out of the routine I was in. My road dog Thomas and I made plans to go check out the city of Songtan, Korea. After I knocked on his door it flew open as if he was standing behind it looking through the peep hole the entire time. "Darkness!" he shouted. This was his normal way of greeting me, and I would always reply with a cutting snarky response myself. Kind of an inside joke we shared due to the extreme differences in skin tone between the two of us. "What's going on man, how you feeling," he asked. "Not much just trying to pick up the pieces and move forward you know? It sucks but hey, it is what it is. At least I can say at the end of the day I did the best I could. Most men who lose their wives usually do something to cause the break up, but I honestly did nothing." I rambled for an hour or so before Thomas finally took advantage of a small break in my story. "Well hey man I don't want to be the bearer of bad news, but I got an email from Tammy a few days ago that was basically asking me to take care of you." "I can show you if you want." "Sure," I said. He opened the email and read it out aloud to make sure I understood the context of the letter.

"Hey please look after Glenn, he and I had some serious problems while he was home on leave. I know it is a bit harsh, but I simply don't want to be married to him any longer. I really tried my best to let him down easy, but it got very ugly. I don't understand why people are pointing the finger at me as if I'm the bad guy. I simply don't want to be married. Anyways, I have to go, please take care of Glenn."

I had to snatch the laptop from him because I thought I was finally getting answers to this divorce debacle. As I read through her venomous filled words, I could also see where he wrote back. *"Tammy you know you really hurt that boy, but don't worry I'll take care of him".* Next was another paragraph from Tammy and from the first sentence, she set the tone for the rest of the email.

"Look a lot of things went down between Glenn and me while he was home. He has some serious issues that he needs to resolve before he can ever imagine us being together. He is very childish and needs to learn how to except the reality of us not being together. I thought I married a man but he is far from that! When things don't go his way it's a problem! I don't hate Glenn, but I am truly fighting the urge everyday as he continues to make me sick with every thought of who he is as a person. I tried my best to make this work, but my heart is not in it anymore. I just want to be left alone. Once again, now that I don't want to be a part of this relationship anymore, everyone is pointing the finger at me as if I'm the bad guy. No one knows my pain... if the world only knew."

I scanned the email once more before I turned to look at Thomas who was trying his best to avoid the conversation. I could see his level of discomfort by this point, since he was now at a loss for words. Hell, I'm not sure what I would have said if the tables were turned. How does a friend truly console another friend after receiving news like I did? He could see the hurt in my face as my eyes filled quickly. "Thomas I have no clue what she's talking about. I'm so confused behind any pain that I caused her. Why is she so disgusted with me? I wish I knew what it was I did wrong, but man trust me when I tell you, I did nothing to hurt her." "I know you didn't man" Thomas replied. "I've known you since you were a private, and I know that when you commit to something, especially a female, you put everything into it. With that being said brother, you are not losing anything more than you are gaining by her leaving you. God knows you did your best to save your marriage, but you can't force someone to be with you who don't want to be. It's her loss because everyone knows you are a good guy and any girl would be lucky to have you."

A few more weeks went by and one day out of the blue I

got a phone call from Captain Chong, the battalion's flight

surgeon. "Hi, can I please speak to Chief Taylor?" asked the

surgeon. "This is he." I said. "Hey Chief, it's Captain. Chong,

how is everything going?" "Fine sir." Instantly I was on the

defense because I didn't know why my flight surgeon was

calling, but I figured it was nothing good. Sure enough he

started the conversation by asking about my vacation and then I

automatically knew he had knowledge of the events that

happened almost two months prior. The thought that I couldn't

shake was why now? It had been nearly two months since I'd

been back in Korea. "Mr. Taylor I received some information

about you while you were home on leave, something about you

spending time in a psychiatric ward." "Well Sir, to give you my

account of what actually happened, because obviously you

received the wrong version. I was forced to spend time in the

hospital after my wife told me she wanted a divorce on my

birthday. This was something that law enforcement made me

do. I had no control over it whatsoever." "Well Mr. Taylor, said the surgeon, until this is straightened out you are hereby medically grounded from flight duty until we can get a psychiatric evaluation done on you. I'm sure you're fine, but in order to make sure all the steps have been taken, an evaluation must be completed."

"Sir, from whom did you get this information?" I asked. "I'm not at liberty to tell you that chief." "So what you're saying is someone has obviously said some things about me that may impact my career, but I'm not entitled to know, ok Sir, that makes sense now, I completely understand." I'm sure by this point he could sense that I was being rather sarcastic and that I was obviously angry about the story he just told me. "Well the information came from a third party who has nothing to do with this case," the surgeon added. "That person is simply acting as a messenger. Now I've already scheduled you for an appointment on the 19th of August." "That's two weeks from now!" I yelled. "Well that's the only opening we have at the moment, I'll let you know if anything opens up between now and then. Have a good day Chief Taylor." He hung up the phone before I could say anything else. This was probably a good thing because I felt as if my tongue was about to slip. "Have a good day Chief Taylor." I could still hear his broken Korean accent playing in my head. "Yeah right" I thought to myself.

The days seemed to drag by. Finally, the day came to see the shrink. To my surprise the doctor began his evaluation just like the Chaplin had a few weeks prior. I almost laughed in his face when he asked me if I was suicidal and homicidal. I quickly controlled the giggles and remembered that I was seeing a psychiatrist this time, not a Chaplin. He may be a little more difficult to convince, so I needed to stay sharp at all times. "So Glenn," said the shrink. "Tell me what brings you here today." "Well sir I had a tad bit of trouble while I was home on leave." "I see," he said. "Please go on." I laid the story down for him just as I did for the Chaplin, but being extra careful as to what I said. By the end of the meeting he not only told me that he believed I was ok, but he also wished he could evaluate Tammy, my soon to be ex-wife. "Glenn, I personally think she is the one that has some serious issues that need to be addressed. Based on the things you have told me I can sense some more complex issues that have not been resolved in her life and unfortunately, you had to reap the consequences of her past. It's common in most women who have had some sort of tragic incidents surrounding a relationship in their past. "You got that right doc, something's definitely off upstairs with her, I just wish I'd known before we got married that she didn't play with a full deck of cards, ya know?"

"Well Glenn, we all make mistakes in life but unfortunately the past is exactly that, moments that have elapsed in our lives that we can never return to. We as human beings may be able to remember distinct details about certain situations, but one thing holds true; we can never alter the events of yesterday, but only use the experience to better prepare ourselves for tomorrow. I know that this was a wakeup call for something tremendous that's about to happen in your life." His words were comforting, but I would soon find out that the context of those words would eventually be a harsh reality.

Later on that day I scheduled an appointment with Captain Chong so I could get back in the air to do what I loved to do, fly. About a week or so passed before I could sit down with him. When I arrived at his office, I wasted no time getting to the point. "Sir I had my session with the shrink, and he signed me off as being fit for flying duty." "I figured he would, said Captain Chong, so here's your paperwork to return to flying status. Just before I reached the handle of the door I pondered on the idea of why this had happened to me, more importantly who was behind it. I stopped in the middle of my tracks and quickly replayed the previous conversation he and I had over the phone. "Sir I've been meaning to ask you where did this all come from?"

"Ok Mr. Taylor, like I told you before it originated from a third party who is completely disconnected from the entire situation." "Who is the third party," I desperately asked. "Look Chief, this is a need to know type situation and you don't need to know!" I stood there in mental shock at what just came out of his mouth but more pissed off at the fact that he wasn't even facing me when he said it. He was deep into his computer screen while I stood behind him deciding if I was going to dive on him or not for the cynical remarks. Smartly, I walked out of the office scheming up other ways to bypass him. He was clearly being protective of someone, but I wanted to know who. I think my motivation was simply to find out who could be trusted and who I needed to be cautious around. What person would take the time to contact someone in Korea and make allegations of me wanting to harm myself or anyone else? Who would know how to reach the appropriate people in order to raise the idea of suspicion? Also, how many people knew about the incident that happened while I was home? If I could answer these three questions I would be well on my way to figuring out who was behind it all. The answer as to who was behind all of this was obvious but I was still in denial. "Damn I married an awful woman," I thought to myself. Back at work things were chaotic around the hanger with an upcoming change of command ceremony. It was time for Major Zackary to move on to bigger and better things in the Army. We would soon be under the command of Major Melody Mitchell. She was previously assigned to the battalion staff and had just been selected from a group of other officers to command the Medevac Company. Just like any other commander in the Army, rumors beat them to the company before they even have a chance to show who they really are. The main rumor that was lurking about Major Mitchell was that she was a hard nose to work for and she was spineless when it came to standing up for her Soldiers. Little did I know then but this would soon prove to be partially true. Later on that week I was scheduled for my first rotation of Medevac duty at Camp Casey. Camp Casey was about a 30 to 35-minute flight north. I was not only thrilled at the idea that I would be pulling duty and responding to real medical emergencies, but I was with one of the coolest pilots in the company. Chad Riggers would be my pilot in command and I had always heard how chill he was to fly with. He was the only guy in the company with a nick name. They called him "Chad Nasty." I never got the meaning of that name or where it derived from, but I can only imagine it revolved around his flying skills. Due to bad weather we drove up to the location where we would be pulling duty. I could tell by the conversation we were having that the rotation would be a good one. The drive lasted about three hours and by the time we got there the weather was clear blue twenty-two.

We relieved the crew that was there, got briefed on new flying hazards in the area and assumed duty. Just moments later the radio operator came dashing down the hall screaming. "Sir, Sir, we have a mission!" The sound of his voice was almost horrifying, but then I remembered this was what I was trained to do; save lives. Chad was on the back stairwell smoking a cigarette when he got the news from the radio operator. I could still hear the sound of urgency in the kid's voice, but it didn't seem to faze Chad at all. He stuck his head in the door and by this time I was struggling to get my gear together for the mission. "Hey Glenn" he said, go get strapped in the aircraft and I'll be there after I finish smoking this cigarette." "Cool, see you in a few" I said. I did as I was told but I must admit that his calmness was a bit disturbing. I kept thinking to myself "there is a man complaining of chest pain who has previously suffered three heart attacks," but Chad had to finish his cigarette or at least this was more important to him. I guess he knows what he's doing I thought. I ran down the hill to the helipad and began the startup procedures by the checklist. A few moments later Chad climbed in the seat beside me, we started the engines, and took off. The adrenaline was incredible. I felt like I was in an action packed movie and had the leading role to save the day. "Balls to the wall man, let's go," Chad instructed. I increased my airspeed and with that, the adrenaline inside of me increased too! Although there was a real emergency going on I was smiling under my sun visor. I must say I felt like a true bad ass. We arrived at the pickup site in less than seven minutes. The flight medic went to assess the patient meanwhile Chad and I sat there waiting on her to return. "Tell me something," I asked. "How can you stay so calm in a situation like this?" Chad chuckled a little bit, exhaled, and said "ya know that's a question I get all the time from brand new pilots. The only thing that I can say is slow is smooth and smooth is fast. It's very important that we as aviators make no mistakes, especially in a critical situation where we are being called upon to be cool under pressure. It takes time but you'll get there too man." A few moments later the flight medic along with a few Soldiers from the site all assisted with loading the patient into the aircraft. We departed shortly thereafter in route to the hospital.

All of a sudden Chad started singing. Al Green's "Let's Stay Together" blared over the headset. I laughed at his version of the lyrics, but more at the fact that it wasn't expected from a man of his color or the lack thereof. We arrived at the hospital helipad before I knew it. I announced I was beginning my approach to the pad. As I was descending I could see Chad smiling out of the corner of my left eye. "What's so funny," I asked. "Nothing brother just watching how tensed you are and remembering I was just like you a few years ago." I cracked a slight smile and refocused my attention on landing the aircraft safely. The medic climbed out of the aircraft to meet the trauma team standing near an ambulance. They strapped the old man in the back of the truck and sped off in route to the hospital. Our job was done and about an hour later we got the news that we saved the old man's life. I felt like a true hero for the first time in my Army career. I had just helped to save a life and was proud to be a part of the crew that day.

I wanted to share the news with someone and honestly brag about how cool my job was. Like a jackass I wrote Tammy an email letting her know about my experience. To this day I'm not sure what was going through my head or why I even attempted to contact her. It had been a few months since our breakup, by this time she was already in Iraq so I figured why not.

"Hey Tammy, I just wanted to stop by, say hello and see how you were doing. I assume you made it safely to your location and you're at work raising hell. Hey if you have your address now please let me know. I would really like to send you some care packages sometime if that's ok with you. The guys at the mail room here felt sorry for me because I never get any mail. They wrote me a note saying "You are not alone sir, we are here with you." They left it in my mailbox along with a candy bar. I thought that was so funny. Anyways as for me, I'm here in the land of confusion taking things one day at a time. I've started taking piano lessons and I think I'm slowly improving. The lady here is really good at teaching and I'm starting to get better at reading music. I'm doing well in my class that I'm taking on line. I remind myself of you I think, I usually have no clue as to what I'm talking about during some of the online discussions, but somehow I still manage to get 100's on my assignments. You must have rubbed off. Flying is getting better for me as well. I had my first three real life missions recently

and the adrenaline is incredible! We received our first call as soon I got on duty a few days ago. This 51 year old man was having severe heart problems so we launched, picked him up, and took him to the hospital, which ultimately saved his life. We had two other missions but not as critical, one kid had a breathing problem and the other had a dislocated shoulder which was more critical due to the flight when we landed. The vibrations of the aircraft didn't help him at all. I kind of felt bad for him. So yeah, I saved at least two lives in a matter of days. That was a great feeling. Well I won't hold you up any longer, just wanted to check in and say hi.

Love, Glenn."

I woke up the next day to a much unexpected email from Tammy especially considering the fact that I wrote nothing mean to her at all.

"Glenn, I'm happy to hear that you are doing well. It's also nice to know that you pursued the piano lessons. We have resources here to purchase things. I sent myself a box of

goodies I needed to get me through the rest of the deployment,
so a care package will not be needed from you. Thank you for
asking though. By the way I called my lawyer, and I want you to
know that I still plan on going through with the divorce. I'm
sure this will not make you happy and personally I could care
less about how you feel. This is something that I need to do for
me; your concerns are not a priority at all. I can't pretend that
nothing happened while you were home and I know that I'm not
happy with you. There is no need for a response from you. Do
us both a favor and delete my contact information and stay away
from me. I wish you all the best, and once again take care!"

After reading the email I remember thinking; I now know who
contacted Captain Chong about the incidents that happened
while I was home on leave for sure! She was more than capable
of knowing how to contact the appropriate people, easily
credible given we were legally still married, and with each email
she showed me just how cold hearted she truly was. The one
question that still ran through my mind unanswered was:

"WHY?"

Chapter 5 "The Wishful Pain Exchange"

The sensation of hurting is a phenomenon that a human being cannot be detached from. This fact is true to all who will experience life, whether in the past, present, or in the future. Pain is the body's response to any type of discomfort either physical or mental. Some individuals however, have overcome this phenomenon and they have replaced the sensation of pain with the feeling of being numb. They are almost dead to the world and all the obstacles that may arise. Some doctors will call this a mental illness because they are not "connected," but is this truly a mental illness? A chemical imbalance in the brain is more than likely the diagnosis they will use. Is this a curse or in fact a gift for those of us who have been through some trouble in our lives? Personally during this time of my life I would have preferred not to feel anything at all and would easily suggest that being numb was the optimum state of mind. To me the thought of being beaten to the brink of losing my life was better than the pain I felt mentally. Personally, I feel as if physical pain is easier to deal with because of the fact that you can watch your wounds heal. With a little time, maybe some medicine and a band aid, your pain will eventually end. Mental pain however, is totally different. You have NO clue when that torment is going to end. I felt as if nothing worse could possibly go wrong in my life. Little did I know, the show was just beginning and I had front row seats.

I believe the saying goes "When it rains it pours," but during this period of my life I was in the middle of a flood without a raft. I had no one to turn to for help and the psychological walls around me were beginning to cave in closer each day until I met Ken, Hakeem, and Raymond. I think they were sent to me as guardian angels, to guide me through the low emotional valleys, and to teach me how to climb life's mountains. Raymond was an old friend I worked with back in Fort Stewart, Georgia and over the years we managed to stay in contact.

We had a similar upbringing considering the fact that his

mother was murdered and his grandmother raised him just like mine. He was a free spirited guy, very easy to talk to, and loved to eat. He maintained a "seefood" diet to the letter and was proud of it. Raymond had a big heart and an even bigger belly. Standing only 5'2", he could easily be picked out of a crowd of people because he resembled a chocolate version of an "umpa lumpa". Ken and Hakeem however, were the complete opposite. They were both pretty stocky guys. Ken could throw up 375lbs in the gym like it was nobody's business. He also had that "don't test me" look on his face all the time. The crazy thing about this is the fact that Hakeem was even more massive than Ken. The guy looked like he ate midgets for dinner and had nails for dessert. Hakeem's statue could easily be compared to Goliath.

He could crush a can of beer between his chest and chin. He's the type of guy I would smartly shoot instead of foolishly engaging in a fist fight. Let's be honest, every now and then you should put your ego in your pocket and walk away.

Hakeem certainly gave people the motivation to do so.

To add to his intimidating demeanor, he was covered in tattoos that started from who knows where, and they ended around his neck with the exception of the three tear drops on his left cheekbone. Hakeem never told us how he got those tear drops or what they meant and I for one wasn't about to ask. Some cans are better left unopened. He spoke with a raspy accent that was a result of smoking black & mild's and cigarettes most of his life. His eyes were always blood shot as if he had spent the previous night drinking himself into oblivion, but this was just his normal appearance. Sometimes I would question how he got in the Army, but let's face it, there's a waiver for everything nowadays.

As scary as he may sound, Hakeem was a pretty chill guy to be around and very wise when it came to lessons of life. A proud brother to the Nation of Islamic faith, he could recite the Quran almost forward and backwards verbatim. Being the asshole friend that I am, I would occasionally invite him to help me cook barbeque ribs and make pulled pork sandwiches just to see how serious he was about Muhammad. That never really went over too well. I was however, able to convince him to visit the church I was attending. Now part of the reason we got along so well was because we were very outspoken people. The filter separator between his brain and his mouth never seemed to work, nor did mine. Whatever was on his mind would soon come out of his mouth. If those around him didn't have tough skin then oh well, or in the words of my darling disaster Tammy, "quit bitching, and keep it moving."

One Sunday after the pastor was done with his sermon, one of the deacons approached me to "share some advice." I stood there quiet and listened to every word that came across his lips. "Brother Taylor I have a revelation from God" he said. He's telling me that you're not trying. I see you sit here every Sunday since your wife left you almost like a zombie. Your body is here, but your mind is somewhere else. God wants you to try and that's the reason why you're going through what you're going through."

I blinked about a 50 times as I watched him dry speckles of undesirable spit from his lips with a handkerchief. I used both hands to loosen the knot in my tie for comfort. He could see me scratch my forehead out of an attempt to hide my face. It's normal for me to laugh out of nervousness or if someone just says something that's flat out stupid. This uncontrollable reaction to foolishness has gotten me into trouble before. It was a habit that I was seriously working on. I do realize that people like to be taken seriously in life, especially when they are trying to "share some advice." I gazed at him while I was still in shock by the things that he just said.

"Hold on brother, let me make sure I understood you correctly. You're telling me that everything I'm going through now is because I'm not trying, is that correct? Well riddle me this deacon, exactly how am I not trying?" He hesitated with his answer probably because he could hear the aggression in my voice and clearly see the anger on my face. Before he could even get another word out I interrupted. "Do you even know what I'm going through deacon?" The sarcasm with the enunciation of the word "deacon" was a verbal spear to his ignorant comment, but yet he had the audacity to keep bumping his damn gums about what he "thought" God told him in a "revelation."

"Well brother that's really none of my business, so no I'm not sure, but it can't be anything worse than what we've all been through." "Oh is that so deacon? I asked. So your wife asked for a divorce on your birthday too?" Little did he know, but this is perhaps my number one pet peeve; people belittling my issues in comparison to their own. People are so quick to point out that things could be so much worse than they are. To me that cliché should be flushed in the deepest toilet on earth because it's worthless. Yes, I would agree that there are people on this earth with serious burdens, but as harsh as it may sound ask yourself this question, "What does that have to do with me?" Your pain will still be there in the morning even after someone uses another person's burdens to try and belittle yours. It seems to me that some people think this is almost a remedy to your troubles. "Oh things could be so much worse they say." To people like that I say go walk across I-95 blindfolded.

"So you don't know what I'm going through I asked the deacon, you're sure it's not as bad as your issues and yet God is telling you that I'm not trying? What's God's phone number maybe we can get him on three-way because that's not what he's telling me?" "Brother Taylor I…" "Deacon Kim enjoy the rest of your evening with your wife and God bless you my brother." I walked out of the church before curse words flew because they were surely dangling on the edge of my soup coolers. It would have been a shame if furniture in the church was rearranged due to me diving on him.

On the way home I told Hakeem what happened and as a result he spent the rest of the ride trying to convince me to turn the car around. He wanted to make his own personal inquiry of exactly what deacon Kim was trying express by telling me that I wasn't trying. I suppressed the raging bull because I could only imagine the story line on the daily news had I turned the car around. It would have probably been something like "Deacon gets a beat down for telling members of the church they are not trying, see page 2." Anyway, a few days went by and I'd finally put the comments behind me from Deacon Kim.

The following Friday afternoon a few of the men from the church decided to get together for some lunch. Before everyone could get there another Deacon from the church said that he had a dream about me the night prior. "Brother Taylor, God was really speaking to me in my heart about you last night while I was dreaming. "Here we go again I thought. I must be the topic of discussion for sure amongst these people who are obviously "holier than thou." "Oh yeah, what was the dream about," I asked. "Well brother Taylor, it was a clear spring day, I could see you and your wife walking together hand and hand on the beach and there was a glow that covered you both like a spiritual vale. I think the point that God showed me is that you have to stop complaining about losing your wife. Every time your mouth opens up it's something about Tammy. He is telling me that he is tired of hearing you complain about her. Every one of us has been through what you're experiencing right now so you really need to stop complaining.

My wife and I were on the verge of divorce just before we got to Korea, but you don't hear me complaining. I busted out and laughed hysterically in his face. He seemed confused by the humor I found in his statement so I explained why I was laughing at him. "So Sunday Deacon Kim told me that God told him I wasn't trying and that's the reason why I'm going through this heartache. Now you're telling me you had a dream God told you that I complain too much about my wife leaving me?" Still in the middle of me laughing I briefly gained control of myself enough to speak.

By this point I was beginning to get fed up with these so called "chosen ones" of the church. I had to let him have it now. "First of all deacon, I'm sure that was gas you felt in your chest during your dream about me and my wife last night, what did you eat for dinner?" "Oh yeah, I added, the fact that you are dreaming about me and my wife being happy together is not a bad thing, but it's just that deacon, a dream." His eyes stretched wide open and his mouth suddenly formed the perfect fly catcher. Shocked was an understatement for his expressions. I guess he didn't know I could flip out the way I did. I can't explain why I got so mad but I just blanked out. My eyes were laser focused on his as I delivered the rest of my deeply buried frustrations. "You lay beside your wife every night and your marriage obviously is a cookie cutter, but you can't understand why I complain so much about a woman I love? You said that you and your wife were on the verge of divorce, but obviously you guys worked through it. Listen Deacon, no offense, but please try to keep us out of your dreams at night. You might want to lay off the Kimchi," I insisted.

"Brother Taylor, there's no reason to get upset, I'm just telling you what God is telling me." "That's just the thing," I said. "God hasn't told me any of that and to be honest with you I truly doubt he spoke to you as well. It seems that you and Deacon Kim both have a special way of hearing the "voice of God," especially when it deals with my life and marriage. The ironic thing is I can never seem to be around when the two of you are receiving these "revelations". "Brother Taylor, I think it would be a good idea if I laid my hands on you and pray for God to take this anger away." I moved my head as he attempted to pray for me in the middle of the food court. It wasn't the fact that I was ashamed of prayer in front of people, but to me it was another blatant attempt to belittle my pain.

As I turned to walk away I could see Raymond and Hakeem walking up to where we were. I felt a bit of relief especially at the fact that Hakeem was there and not just Ray. I guess they both could sense something was wrong given the awkward silence from the deacon.

"Everything ok?" Hakeem asked as he glared at the deacon. The look on his face helped to remind me of exactly how crazy he was. The gaze in his eyes said it all. Suddenly I remembered the intensity of the conversation between Hakeem and I about last Sunday. "I hope he doesn't say anything crazy to this guy", I thought. Maybe it was just me, but I couldn't help but think something bad was about to happen. So there we were, Hakeem laser focused on the deacon as if he was waiting on him to make a faulty move and me standing there in the middle to resolve anything that might happen. Raymond was distracted with other priorities as he scurried over to order a bucket of chicken big enough to feed a small village in Africa. "Damn that guy can eat," I thought. "Yeah everything is ok Hakeem, I was just leaving."

I gently nudged Hakeem towards the line that Raymond was standing in. This was my successful attempt to rectify a probable incident between the deacon and Hakeem. I could only imagine what would have been said had I not gotten him away from the deacon. I remind you again that Hakeem's verbal filter separator did not work properly, nor did mine. This pretty much meant an F bomb would fly at the drop of a dime from the both of us. All it took was a little stupidity to set either of us off.

When we got in the line behind Raymond we both couldn't help but to laugh at his order. I think the cashier even got a kick out of it too, especially after I added the fact that the meal was just for him alone and no one else. She bit her bottom lip to keep from smiling. "So that's a 20-piece mixture of spicy chicken, 4 apple pies, and a large diet coke?" she asked. "Yes ma'am," Raymond replied. "Make sure that's a diet coke and not a diet Pepsi," he added. "Damn Ray, are you really about to smash that entire bucket of chicken," Hakeem asked. "Yes sir," Ray replied. "It's about to get real serious between me and this poultry. That being said fellas, I would highly advise you to ask any questions that you may have for me now or leave them for the end. Bottom line, don't speak to me while I'm eating." "Ok Ray, enough with the shenanigans," I said. We all sat down at a table that was adjacent to the TV so we could catch the game while we ate. The Lakers were beating the brakes off of the Spurs. The game wasn't much of a game at all and it appeared that San Antonio needed to saddle up and ride off into the sunset back to Texas.

"What was the deacon talking to you about," Raymond asked. "Oh that was another so called revelation that he wanted to share. Supposedly in a dream last night God told him to tell me that I complain too much about losing my wife. I never knew people in the church could gossip so damn much. It's clear that I'm a topic of discussion amongst them, but I wish they would stop using God's name in vain. I mean let's be real about it I've heard of women gossiping here and there, but that's part of their nature. The same is true for ladies going to the bathroom together and forgetting to look before they sit on a toilet seat. My point is by the way these two bozos have been acting in the past week or so, it wouldn't surprise me if they sit while they piss side by side in bathroom stalls. I can only envision the things they whisper about me to each other. By this point

Hakeem had cooled off and was actually laughing hysterically at my remarks about the two deacons. A moment of silence awkwardly joined the three of us at the table. While sitting there I began to reminisce on a child hood quote that my grandmother preached to my sister Bianca and I, she would tell us "Always remember to take six months to mind your business and another six months to stay out of everyone else's."

Chapter 6 "Sweet Marie"

I think it's fair to say there comes a point in every bad break up where sooner or later; we just have to say the hell with it! There's no point in fighting any longer for a person who won't fight for you. This is especially true if it's clear that they are fighting against you instead of with you. After the malicious emails from Tammy subsided I fell into an even darker place emotionally. That's when I think I stopped caring shortly thereafter. Given the circumstances that had taken place you would think I would have been over her a long time ago, but I wasn't.

When a man loves a woman he does whatever it takes to make her smile, keep her secure within the relationship, and ultimately treat her like a queen. That love doesn't die or go away over night, but days turned into weeks and weeks into months. The chances of any type of reconciliation between Tammy and I became as unrealistic as seeing the color of love. I would spend hours at a time wondering if true love really existed. Ken and his wife was one of the only couples that showed each other true love, so I naturally favored their friendship. One day, Ken and I went out to dinner with some of his friends from the office. After we all made some wise decisions that ended up at the bottom of a shot glass, we went our separate ways from the group.

The following morning we got up for our usual workout session. The gym was never packed that early in the morning and we could pretty much use whatever equipment we wanted. I stretched my arms by dangling from a pull-up bar. "Man that feels good" I said as I dropped down from my dangling stretch. By this point Ken was finishing the last strap on his glove. We started with a light chest warm up as it was going to be the area of concentration that day.

This was probably the best mental outlet I could have used while I was in Korea. It's crazy how working out can actually become addictive. We spent the next hour or so doing repetitious exercises. After working our usual chest and abs, Ken and I decided to play a game of one on one. The basketball court was empty for the most part with the exception of a hot brunette working on her jump shot. Ken started a game of horse with a free throw that I matched a minute later. About midway into our game with a shift of his eyes and a nod of his head, he redirected my focus towards the girl who was only a few feet away.

"Baby girl is undressing you with her eyes," he whispered. I denied his remarks and down played the conversation with a fast response of my own. "If she's looking at anyone she's looking at you, playa." We both laughed, but then I noticed that his assumption was spot on. I glanced at her once and then again to make sure I wasn't fooling myself. Both times we locked eyes and then quickly looked away like two pimpled faced kids on a playground. A few moments later she came over to where we were.

"Excuse me she finally asked, but do you know who I

need to speak to about joining the female basketball team?" "I'm not sure I replied, but I may be able to get some information, hang on a second." I walked over to my gym bag to get my phone, as I turned I noticed Ken had a big grin all over his face. I bit my lip to keep from smiling myself. After a few calls to some friends I scored the number for a guy named "slim". "Hey give this guy a call," I said. He's the head coach here on base. His name is "slim," but he reminds me of a baby orca, you'll see why when you meet him. She chuckled at my joke and then asked if she could have my number in case any other "issues" came up. Reading between the lines I said "sure, 010-3272-5573, hit me up whenever." "I most definitely will," she said. "Thanks again." Later on that night I got a text from a number that wasn't in my phone.

Thank you so much for helping me earlier. You are so sweet.

You're welcome, whoever you are...Lol

It's Marie the girl from the gym earlier today☺

Oh, Hi how are you?

I'm ok just got out of the shower

Good. Stay fresh...lol

Lmao, always boo boo ☺

"That's the second smiley face she's sent in the past thirty seconds," I thought to myself. Then the visual slapped me without warning. I was on the phone with a wet brunette if you recall she told me that she just got out of the shower. What was the purpose of the smiley face? Besieged with curiosity after the last text message, I played into her game. After an hour of texting back and forth we called it quits for the night. I had to be up at five and she mentioned some sort of formation she had to go to as well. A few days later while walking through the Post Exchange I heard a voice say "hey stranger." Turning to look I quickly noticed a more fixed up version of Marie. Her hair was pressed neatly down her back. The makeup she wore was perfectly placed as if she spent the entire morning doing it or had it done by a professional. The scent of candy wrapped around her person. I cracked a slight smile in an attempt to hide my initial thought which was DAMN! I couldn't believe this was the same girl from the gym.

"Hey how have you been? Did you ever get in contact with the coach about joining the team?" "Yes, I had my first practice on Monday and we already have a game coming up this Saturday." "Cool well hey I have to get going, I've been shamming out of work for the past hour or so." As I turned to walk away she grabbed my arm. "Hey before you go, I would love to invite you to my first basketball game." I paused while my mind briefly went on a voyage. Was this just an innocent invitation to a basketball game or was it in fact an invitation for me to drop my balls in her basket after the game? Only time would tell but I had the feeling the latter was promising.

At the game later on that weekend I sat and watched as the Osan Tigers ripped a new hole into the Humphrey Falcons. The score at the final buzzer was 96 to 12. As I walked out Marie caught my attention from amongst the group of girls standing by the bleachers. She mouthed the words "I'm going to call you later." I gave her the quick north and south nod of my head and walked out of the double gym doors. Twelve minutes after ten my phone ringed as promised. It was Marie asking me to scoop her up because she was feeling down about the loss her team just took.

By this point in my life and especially in the smoldering stages of my dissolving marriage I was more than happy to cheer her up after that loss. I picked her up and the night began from there. We drove straight to my place. "Hey I don't like a lot of people in my business," I said. Take this key, go up the steps through that side door and my room is the first one on the left; apartment 416." "Anything for you sweetheart I mean you did show up to my game for me."

She said this flirtatiously enough for me to blush before she got out of the car. I parked in the garage across the street and grabbed the spare key out of the center console. I guess she could hear me fumbling outside of my door so before I could even use the key card she snatched it open. She had already taken her shoes off and helped herself to a drink.

"I hope you don't mind," she said as she sipped from a familiar looking can, "but I jacked your last grape soda from the fridge." "Well that's usually grounds for a well whooped ass but I'll make an exception for you I guess." I gave her a small tour of my apartment and then we flopped down on the standard military issued sofa. It was only big enough for the two of us so I figured I would be a smart ass and make a clever comment as I turned on the TV. "You know you have to be in love to sit on this love seat right?" "Well maybe that's something we can work on together" said Marie.

I laughed at her but more at myself for even using the word, "love" considering my recent encounter with the virus. I quickly changed the subject. "So have you been playing ball for a while," I asked. "Yeah I played in college." "Really what position?" "I played point guard and center." "So you're pretty good at using your body to get the job done huh?" "Yep" said Marie. For some reason I was nervous but the flirty comments between the two of us seemed to come natural and they only got better as time passed.

"So tell me something," I whispered. "Yeah what's up?" "What's with you undressing me with your eyes the other day instead of just coming over to talk to me?" "No I wasn't!" "Yeah well there are two against one. Remember my boy Ken," I asked. "Umm… yeah big black guy right?" "Yeah that's him. He was the one who caught you first and then me." "What can I say, you're a pretty good looking man" said Marie. I could only hope that she wasn't looking for a compliment in return because I for one was playing hard to get.

"Who's that in the painting," Marie asked as she pointed towards a picture frame that was facing the opposite direction under my kitchen table. "That's Hitler's adopted daughter." "What are you talking about," Marie asked. "That's my soon to be x-wife, Tammy. "Oh I see. You're crazy for comparing your wife to Adolf Hitler." I maintained a straight face while trying to understand the humor behind the reference to my estranged wife. I seriously felt that my description was spot on. When she noticed my face was straight as a board, she stopped smiling and quickly changed her tone of voice. "So you guys are having problems," Marie asked. "Typical Army marriage I mumbled" as I reached for the TV controller.

"She doesn't look like a bad girl; not bad at all if you ask me. She looks like an angel in this picture. You just sound like a VERY bitter man." "Marie you wouldn't believe my story even if you were strapped down to a table and forced to read it." "Try me," she shouted with a bit of excitement in her voice. "It's really a long story; we'll be here half the night." "I've got time, she insisted. I told my roommate I'd probably be out for the rest of the night, so she won't be expecting me back." I was quiet for a minute while my imagination painted a picture for "the rest of the night." Over the next hour or so I explained the entire situation with Tammy.

"Glenn that is so sad. I really hate she did that to you. Some women don't know what they have until they lose it." "I know but none of that is a concern to her and she could care less about how I feel. That's why I've decided to do my own thing. I'm entirely too young to sit here and stress out over a woman who wants nothing to do with me. It's time to move on; I just haven't found the right girl to move on with."

"Well then, she said. Like my mom has always told my older brother, the quickest way to get over a woman is under another woman." She crossed her legs over my lap which triggered a sensation I couldn't control. I did everything in my power to restrain my inner warrior but I guess it was a lost cause because after a few minutes she asked… "What's that in your pocket?" I stayed quiet while observing the curvature of her lips, the lust in her eyes and completely ignored her question. "What's your favorite chocolate bar," I asked. "I have a few" but hands down I love snickers!" Once again being the smart ass that I am I took advantage of a moment of mockery. "Well if you're hungry why wait?" She smiled slick and sly from the corner of her left eye as if she couldn't believe the words that came from my mouth but you could tell she secretly hoped they were true. Obviously overwhelmed with the tingling sensation from her under carriage, she took another sip of her soda in an attempt to gain her composer. She bit her smile only to have it dissolve into a lustful gaze. "Does that tell you enough about what's in my pocket," I asked.

"No it doesn't she said boastfully, I need a closer look." "I thought you would never ask," I said. She ripped open my candy wrapper and began to indulge for the comfort of her sweet tooth. With elegant precision she did everything to prove to me that she was in fact a head strong lady. While slightly on the brink of a concussion from the continuous pounding of her forehead against my abdomen, the "rest of the night" was just beginning as I started to explore the depths of her canvas. "It's been a while since I've had a king size" she said. I reassured her that it was incredibly bad manners to speak with her mouth full. Demanding more of my sweetness, she led me to the center of her universe. Obliged by her generosity, I started to knock on the bottom of her basement. While vocalizing her confessions, she screamed my name as I reconstructed her floor boards. After vigorously searching for her goal, she digested the seeds of my future. Together we cleansed the sweat of our passion and fell into a deep coma like sleep.

Chapter 7- "The ride to remember"

The next weekend was a four-day weekend and that gave my friend Dwayne and I time to make some less than legal traveling plans. Considering the mile radius that we were supposed to stay within, traveling to Busan, Korea was a blatant act of disobedience but the rules always seemed to be bent when I was with Dwayne. We both had the same mentality as to how we were being treated as pilots in the unit. Basically neither one of us would kiss the commander's ass in order to gain favor for flight time. It's sad to say, but the unit we were in was definitely one of those "good old boy" organizations.

So there we were in Dwayne's third new car after only a few months in Korea. Needless to say Dwayne had sore luck when it came to finding a descent ride to scoot around in. This one seemed to be holding up as Dwayne hauled ass down the highway. I held on for my life as I screamed for Dwayne to snap out of his NASCAR seizure. "Dwayne what's the rush," I shouted. "It's a five and a half -hour trip Glenn, no time to waste. We got to get there so we can get twisted, hit some clubs for free if we can, and sip some more drinks like the true rock stars we are. Remember that night of our flight school graduation" Dwayne asked, while cracking a devilish grin.

"How could I forget Dwayne? The next morning, I woke up in a bowl of ramen noodles and chicken bones stuck to a remnant of an ATM receipt from Teasers. Trust me Dwayne, I remember. It's spotty here and there, but I do remember the receipt was for $260.00, so I can only imagine what we got into." "Was 'Luscious Lemon Drop' working that night, he asked. I can't remember?" "I'm not a stripper groupie, I said. Nor do I pay for my love by the hour like you." "What's that supposed to mean?" he asked. "I don't know any strippers, especially on a first name basis." Later on that night my dear friend Dwayne decided that it would be cool to play a drunken game of hide and seek. The only difference between Dwayne's version and the traditional version is that normally the game ends within a matter of minutes. By this point Dwayne was gone for an hour. The last I saw of him was just before I left to pee. This was Dwayne's second disappearing act since we'd become pilots. Just a year or so prior to this night he pulled another stunt just like this while we were still in flight school. There I sat alone at the bar only imagining where my friend might be. Searching for him would have been the same as using a condom with a hole in it; a waste of time.

Another hour passed and there still was no sight of Dwayne. "Where did your friend go" asked the bartender. "I'll be damned if I know your guess is as good as mine." "Well don't just sit here she insisted, you should go dance with the pretty girls." "You know, that doesn't sound like a bad idea at all." Dancing has always been a forte of mine and after throwing back a few drinks my abilities increase. I danced with a few ladies through the club, but the chemistry was lacking with each girl so I soon returned to my bar stool with hopes of my friend resurfacing. Shareese and I met shortly after I made it back to the bar. After a night of dancing and drinking liquid courage, the two of us apparently needed to refuel. "What can I get for you" the bartender asked with a broken English accent. "Budweiser," I said. As soon as the bartender turned to grab my beer, Shareese lit a cigarette and blew smoke as she smiled at me. She walked over to my side of the bar to say hello. I extended my hand and clutched her palm inside of mine. "My name is Shareese" she screamed as the sounds of Latin music blared through the speakers in the club. I smiled and said hello as I tickled the center of her palm with the tip of my index finger. "You certainly know what you're doing on the dance floor. I've never seen a straight man with moves like you. You are straight right?" I smiled through a blush which inevitably ignited the conversation. "I'm straight as a drill tip" I replied, while leaving her with a real tip as to maybe drilling **HER** later on that night.

"That's nice to know, so what are you drinking?" she asked. "A nice cold beer" *because you deserve what each*
-

individual _should_ _enjoy_ _regularly._ After seeing the confusion on

her face I quickly explained my play on letters with the word

"Budweiser". "That's slick" she said while flicking her ashes

from the end of her cigarette. "So how can I be as lucky as some

of these other girls you've been dancing with tonight." "Just say

the word sweetie and I'll sweep you off your feet." She guzzled

the last gulp from her martini and chewed the green olive that was

at the bottom of the glass.

Song after we danced as if we had known each other for

years. The night evolved with the two of us sharing a cab back

to my hotel. We'd plan on sitting up talking, sharing stories

about life, and eating some food to help sober up. Well once we

were inside the cab Shareese fell asleep with her head in my lap.

I passed out as well but I was soon awakened by the knowledge

she started to share with me in the back of the taxi. Impressed

by her skills to grab the bull by the horn I captured the moment

for what it was.

With the slightest concern about the driver of the taxi, Shareese began to embark upon her unyielding desire. "This is very different; I've never done it in a taxi she slurred while gagging herself violently; but I am an agent of change." She took off her glass stripper heels and pulled her panties aside, separating her soft pink passion with the tips of two moistened fingers. Without a shadow of doubt she granted me "access," to feel what she wanted to "express," from the southern end of her little, tight, black dress. Armed with the proper lifestyle, my Trojan was beyond ready for battle in Shareese's sweet vertical valley. The cab driver chuckled as he approached the last light before our final destination.

She rode the bull until we reached the front of the hotel lobby. I was certain we were going to jail for the crime of passion committed in the backseat of the cab. Fortunately for us the driver was cool about Shareese's academy award winning performance. I paid him 50,000 Korean won as a token of my appreciation. When I woke up the next morning,

Shareese was still down for the count. Her hair covered the pillow and formed a silky trail down to the center of her spine. My eyes were then afforded the opportunity to identify her tramp stamp which read, "these two holes are for you." Below the stamp there was the stem of a rose pointing to her two options of sexual satisfaction.

Captivated by the sight of her sweet thighs, my third leg began to rise. I guess she could feel me fumbling around, so she pulled the sheets which were covering her legs and turned over to face me. This woman was very beautiful, even in the morning, but her breath was nothing cute. I could have won an award for best "kiss dodger" considering my efforts to beat the "heat." I used the excuse of going to the bathroom as a means to get away from Shareese's mouth. I drained the main vein, washed my hands, and walked out with my toothbrush in my mouth. My hopes were that she would ask if I had an extra toothbrush; that way I could avoid any other clever tactics. Fortunately for me it worked.

The two of us both agreed to never drink around each other again because of the possibility that another "ride to remember" would take place. Who knows where it might have happened, not to mention the fact that we were both legally married. I guess there was a breach of our contract, because the floor was suddenly the surface of an encore. With her face down and her ass up, I cracked the cookie and started reminding her of the bright future behind her. The events continued as she defied gravity in my arms while we both gazed upon a lustful reflection in the mirror. I watched as she bit her bottom lip and caught a glimpse of myself with licentious rage on my face. Pausing only to reposition, we continued to punish each other for the next 69 minutes. She rode me hasty as I drove her crazy. After she was well disciplined, we finished our display of acrobatics with her savoring my flavor. I wondered if it would have been appropriate to applaud or perhaps assist with the cleanup of a sticky situation. That was the one and only occasion Shareese and I wet the sheets together. Time passed and the friendship became strictly platonic, weird considering how it started. I guess the guilt between the two of us took its toll even with her having troubles with her husband and me still confused as to what happened with my wife.

Chapter 8- Oct 14th

It's funny how we as men usually turn to one or two things when a woman we love leaves us; the bottom of a bottle or perhaps the bottom of another woman. I turned to both. In hindsight this was definitely the wrong means to handle the birthday gift from Tammy. Sexual healing was only a Band-Aid for the puncture wound left in my heart. Despite the sweet sensation from Marie's southern comfort and a ride to remember with Shareese, I would still reminisce the times that Tammy and I were actually on good terms. The questions that developed in my mind were endless, but one particular question always resurfaced; that being how did this all happen so fast?

One Friday night I was awakened to the sound of water dripping in my kitchen sink. I've always been a pretty light sleeper; the sound of a mouse fart is enough to wake me up. So it's needless to say the sound of this drip was drowning the dreams I desired. I tossed and turned until finally I caught myself staring at the ceiling in the midst of darkness. The blinds above my bed revealed a passage of light from the post outside my window. My eyes traced the edges of a letter written by my once beloved. It was stuck in the middle of a book which laid upon the dusty window ceil. I sat up and began to recall the sounds of Tammy's voice as I read.

1/15/11

Hello Baby!

> *I pray that this letter finds you in high hopes. Marrying you was one of the best decisions I have ever made in my life. I don't regret a single moment of the time we've been together. I love you with all of my heart and I would never do anything to hurt you. I meant every word that I said in my vows to you. I will love you and only you for all of the days of my life. I miss you already and it's only been a short spell. You are everything that I have ever wanted in a man. You're beautiful inside and out. I can't wait to come to Korea so I can be in your arms again. I love you Glenn Taylor!*

Love,

Tammy Taylor.

It's puzzling how she could have written something so *heartfelt* and yet only a few months later, send emails that were so *heartless*. There were a few I deleted, but I saved the ones that I thought would eventually resurface during the course of the divorce. For instance, there's one particular letter from her that will always linger in my mind. The subject line stated "Keep testing me"

7/20/11

"I spoke to my mom this morning and she told me that you have been calling. Do NOT call my mother or send my daughter mail again! You are a child and you need to act like an adult. I can't wait to divorce you and be rid of you forever. I told my mom not to talk to you or put Ashley on the phone with you. We are not getting back together and I don't want to even see your face. You need not respond because this is my last time talking to you about this. If you keep this up I will go to the police and file harassment charges. Leave me and my family the hell alone! You are pathetic and you need to move on! I can't wait for this divorce to be finalized so I can no longer be burdened by you or your last name. You are trapped inside of a 12 year old kid's head. No one in my family can help you Glenn, and all you are doing is making yourself look like a jack ass.

Leave my family alone!

P.S. I also informed my commander of this so don't be surprised if your commander speaks with you soon!

Sure enough my commander did speak to me, but definitely not on the terms Tammy would have hoped for I suppose. After another sleepless night amongst the many that would surely follow, I was ordered to report to the commander's office at 0900 hours. I arrived at the parking lot of the company at a quarter till. The CV axle on my car clicked loud enough to scare away a stray dog as I squeezed into the parking spot. I turned the ignition switch off which somehow or another caused my windshield wipers to sway from left to right. The engine sputtered slowly until it finally decided to stop running. This was the usual occurrence upon exiting my vehicle. When I approached the turnstile gate my mind began to race with thoughts of the worst. The handle to the company door was snatched out of my hand by my platoon leader. I could tell something was up by the look on his face. Lieutenant Chisholm was one of the best platoon leaders I'd ever had. He was the type of guy that you actually wanted to work for; not to suck up to him for brownie points or anything like that, but he was just different from the typical Lieutenant. At the threshold of the door his face painted a somber picture creating more suspense on my part.

"Sir what's wrong," I asked. "Let's step outside," he said. I reached for my hat that I had just stowed away in my cargo pocket. We walked side by side to the edge of the smoke

pit; my head was bent low enough to trace the silhouette of my

shadow. I anticipated the worst as we came to a halt. "Listen

Glenn," he said soft spoken and lucid, "Major Mitchell received

an email from your wife's commander today. He said that you

have been harassing her and that it's starting to affect her work

performance." I cracked a slight smile as I shook my head in

disbelief. Not only was this a lie, but it was a cry for attention

if you ask me. As we stood there by the smoke pit I briefly

glared off into space. The sun beamed down on the both of us

from the rear of the maintenance hangar. I cleared my throat

before I replied to make certain that I was being taken seriously.

"Sir, I haven't spoken to my wife in over four months," I

said. "I'm here in Korea and she's in Iraq. How could I possibly

be harassing her from here,." Lieutenant Chisholm lowered his

head revealing a spot of thinning black hair as he remained quiet.

"Glenn listen, I'm only trying to give you a heads up. I'm just a

messenger. The commander knows about the nasty divorce that

you are going through; she's only concerned about your well-being. She only wants to talk to you to make sure you're doing ok." As we turned to walk back to the office, a gust of wind cooled the sweat from the collar of my shirt. I could hear the sound of a fork lift in the distance accompanied by the rumble of helicopters close by. Lieutenant Chisholm reached for the handle of the door and motioned me with his hand to walk in first. "After you," he said. "Thanks Sir is she ready for me now?" Just as he started to answer, the commander opened the door to her office. "Mr. Taylor," she said, "C'mon in, I've been expecting you." She led the way as the three of us walked into her office. I stood in front of her desk at the position of attention; head straight, shoulders back, legs slightly locked together rigidly. As I raised my hand to salute she interrupted. "Relax," she said, "have a seat." The two of us did as we were told, I sat in the chair closest to the wall and Chisholm took the one by the door.

As Lieutenant Chisholm retrieved a pad to take notes, Major Mitchell reached to turn off the loud oscillating fan that stood in the corner. "Mr. Taylor, as I'm sure you already know, I received an email from your wife's commander earlier this morning. I wanted to let you know firsthand because I know how difficult a time like this can be." "I really appreciate that," I quickly replied. "Are you familiar with your wife's commander at all, she asked. His name is Captain Clitoriley, ever heard of him?" "No ma'am," can't say that I have." "Well according to him, you have been harassing your wife, I'm not sure how you have the time or the ability to do so, but this is what was said. He requested that I issued a no contact order that would restrict you from speaking to her. Mr. Taylor I denied his request under the legal circumstances that you two are still married. You should be able to communicate with your wife whenever you so please, especially if there's a chance that you two might work your problems out." "Ma'am, with all due respect, I replied. I'm confident at this point in our relationship we'll never get back together." "Well then, said Major Mitchell, I won't hold you up any longer; get back to work, that's all I have for you. Once again, I just wanted to inform you of this situation. Stay strong Mr. Taylor, and remember that you are my only concern," she concluded. "Thanks ma'am" I said, as I rendered a quick hand salute before leaving her office.

The following weekend was slow to arrive after a stressful work week. The heartbreaking idea of losing my wife soon turned into the spell of a curse. Oppressed by the barriers of distance from my family, and a lack of ability to resolve any of the issues in my marriage, I sought after a common remedy to life's discomfort. Hours later I found myself at "3 Stooges," a local bar in the village outside of the camp. Colorful lights flashed to the rhythm of music as I sipped on the stiff taste of a crown and coke. I turned to face the dance floor while swallowing the last drop of my drink. There I sat alone as I gazed at the people in the crowd; all of them were dancing, smiling, and having a great time. The feeling of misery began to swarm my mind as time passed. Overwhelmed with the mismatched building blocks of mixed emotions, I paid the tab

and left the bar. There was a strip of clubs throughout the village

where most Soldiers hung out on the weekends. I passed a few,

but the drinks from the previous bar led me to a club called "All

Stars." This hole in the wall was built like a two story motel.

When I got to the top of the steps there was a wooden door that

granted access into the club. I looked around the walls until I

spotted a sign above the restroom. It was almost like my bladder

knew I was getting closer to a urinal, the pressure worsened as I

fumbled with my zipper. With the sound of techno music

muffling from inside the club, I faintly heard the voice of a

stranger, or at least I thought she was. "Excuse me," said the soft

voice from the depths of a drunken soul, can't you see someone

is in here asshole?" I turned to look at the curtain that was

separating the urinal from the toilet. Almost all of the clubs in

the village had unisex bathrooms so I was lost for words as I

stood there fumbling with my pants. "Sorry ma'am, I replied,

please forgive me; didn't mean to come barging in here on you like that, I do apologize."

"You could have knocked," the voice said. What kind of a jerk are you, she asked. Once again I tried to resolve the situation kindly. "Listen ma'am, I've already apologized for walking in on you, just give me a second to wash my hands and I'll be out of here." "Wait a minute…Glenn is that you," the voice asked. Startled that my voice was recognizable, I hesitated to respond. "Who is that," I asked. "It's me Elena," she said as the sound of the lid slammed down on the toilet. The dark curtain fluttered from her movements on the other side. As I started to wash my hands she finally revealed herself from behind the curtain. She wore a black blouse, some white yoga pants, and furry boots that had two little dangling balls from the top of her laces. The paper towels were missing from the holder so I dried my hands on my jeans while Elena stood only a few feet away. Truly embarrassed for walking in on her, I started apologizing once again. "I'm so sorry for busting in here like that," I said. "It's ok, but you're lucky we're friends," she flirted. "We are still friends," she asked with the look of erotic curiosity glistening in her eyes.

I cracked a slight smile out of mere discomfort then giggled a little in an attempt to wander. She raised her eye brows which seemed to demand an answer. The words in my head were completely different from what I wanted to say, but considering the situation I bit my tongue for the sake of peace. "Elena we can always be friends, just friends though," I added. "I know we have had our fair share of flirting in the past, but we have to leave it at that. The devious smile that she once wore began to fade away.

The music in the background broke into a moment of silence as the song playing came to an end. Elena stood there somber and motionless as I reached for the handle of the door. Just before I pulled the door open she interrupted yet again. "Wait she said, hang on a second." When I turned to face her the disappointing look of sorrow had been replaced with a glare of seduction. "Can I at least have a taste," she whispered while slowly glancing beneath my waist. I chuckled slightly and scratched

my forehead in disbelief. "Goodnight Elena, be sure to wash

your hands," I uttered before opening the door of the latrine. I

left her standing there beside the stall only to walk out to a girl

dancing on the bar at the front of the club. Three G.I.'s sat and

watched as she dazzled their imaginations with deliberate

gestures. I laughed a little as I walked back down the steps

leading to the cobble Stone sidewalk. "Only in Korea," I

thought to myself as the reality of Elena's bathroom proposal

started to home in. How ironic I thought. Out of all the women

in the village I could have met, I bumped into Elena inside of a

bathroom.

When I turned the corner adjacent to the strip of clubs I

saw a local vender prepping buns for cheeseburgers. The aroma

from the grill swam through the air as I passed by. I watched as

the smoke rose up through the air and dissipated in front of a

partially lit neon sign. "Cheese burger Sir?" asked the local

villager in an attempt to gain a sale. "No thanks Sir, I'm good,"

I said as politely as I could. The music continued to boom in the distance as I approached the last block on the street. The traffic was heavy as usual with taxies passing by as I stood there and waited for my time to cross. From the corner of my left eye I noticed a girl and a guy leaving a cell phone store. Soldiers shopped there all the time because it was across the street from the front gate of camp. The sound of bells clanged against the glass door as it closed shut behind them. I casually refocused my attention back to the traffic passing by. The chatter between the two of them grew as they walked up closer to where I was. The guy was a bit husky and he appeared to be about five feet or so as he barely stood over the top of the female with him. His eyes were dark brown and his skin was a pale white complexion. "I'll ask him," said the girl while pointing her thumb in my direction. "Let's just go," said the guy as he seemed irritated with his friend. Despite his efforts she moved in closer to me. Her small statue was engulfed with the scent of cheap perfume and hairspray. She looked up at me with some of the bluest eyes

I think I have ever seen in my life. "Excuse me," said the girl, "can you help me please? My name is Chrissie; I have a birthday coming up on Monday so my friends decided to throw me a little party tonight. Two of them are moving back to the states and they both wanted to do something for me before they leave next week." By this point I could feel my eye brows rising on the top of my forehead as I listened. "OK," I said, clearly portraying my confusion. "I'm a little drunk, she continued and I heard the guards were giving breathalyzers at the gate." I opened my arms relaying a clueless resolution. "I really don't know what to tell you," I said as the three of us crossed the street between a small break in traffic. "Well can you go ahead of us," she asked. Maybe they won't bother me if I'm in between the two of you, she added as she pointed towards her friend. I briefly pondered on the idea of me being in her shoes when I was twenty. I thought of the true fact that Soldiers are old enough to risk their lives for our country, but not old enough to have a few drinks. Feeling a bit of empathy for Chrissie and her friend, I gave in to her plea. "Ok listen," I said, I don't know you and you don't know me. I'll walk in front of you, but if you get popped I have nothing to do with it." "Thank you soooo much," she cried as she interlaced her fingers in a posture of prayer. "One more thing," she said, can I have your number just in case." "Sure, I replied, with no intentions of ever speaking to her again, 010-3272- 5573." I could feel my phone vibrating inside my back pocket as her call came through. "Got it," I said. When we walked through the gate there was nothing out of the ordinary, the guards were simply checking ID cards as usual and the traffic of people was in a continuous flow. I instantly noticed my unit was running a fundraiser as the three of us walked through the gate. The sound of rock music accompanied with casual conversations could be heard as we finally said our goodbyes and went separate ways. "Thanks for helping us," said Chrissie, while walking in the opposite direction towards a cab. I shot a quick peace gesture in the air with no words spoken replying in silence.

I can still recall the scent of grilled food swarming through the air just before my first sergeant spoke to me. "What's up chief," he asked, filled with energy and perhaps a bit of false motivation. "We got these hotdogs and hamburgers for sale, all donation based he added. I know how much you love to eat, sir." I rubbed my belly as if I were starving and agreed with him. The truth was I wasn't hungry at all, but I just wanted to support the company event. I fixed myself two hotdogs and grabbed a soda from the bottom of a Styrofoam cooler. The cold water sent a shocking chill through my hand as I reached for the can under the ice. The event was donation based, so I gave the last bit of money in my wallet and attempted to say my goodbyes. I started to walk through the path that would have eventually led to my apartment, but I was stopped once again by the first sergeant. "Ah sir, do you have a ride," he asked. "Oh it's not that far, I replied. Plus I've had a few," I said while rocking my thumb and pinky to imitate a beer up to my lips. "I'm just gonna step it out to my room," I replied. "Sir I can give you a ride, he offered. Just hang on a minute; I'm parked across the street." I stood there at the beginning of the trail that had been made into a path from other Soldiers taking the same route home. A few moments later the first sergeant pulled his car up against the side of the curve in front of the patio. I hopped in and we took off towards my place. The conversation between the two of us was casual during the five-minute drive to my building. When we pulled up he parked on the side that allowed easy access to my room. The elevator in the lobby of the building creaked as it came to a halt at the bottom floor. I kicked my shoes off as soon as I opened the door and helped myself to another drink from the top of my kitchen cabinets. An hour or so passed and after a few more shots I was drunk off my ass. My phone rang from the same pocket as I had obviously forgotten to take it out earlier. The number wasn't saved, but out of curiosity I answered. "Hello," I said while lying in the middle of my living room floor. "Can you come over," said the voice of a girl, clearly and precise." Without even inquiring as to who I was speaking to in my drunken state, I went along with the proposal from the girl on the other end of the line. Five minutes didn't elapse before my phone was going off again, but this time in the form of a text message that read "HOW BIG IS IT?" Before I could reply with the 12-inch response, my phone began to ring. "Where are you, she asked, I want you inside of me so bad it hurts," she added. "See you in a few I said, control that fire until I'm there to put it out properly. She sighed and exhaled in a frustrating grunt. "Hurry up." Moments later my cab finally pulled up in front of her building. I paid for the taxi with a bunch of coins inside of a plastic Tupperware bowl. I stood and watched the brake lights of the cab as it approached the stop sign at the end of the block. The cab driver departed the intersection as I texted the mystery number inside of my phone. "I'm outside of your place," I typed, only to receive an immediate response in the spare of a few seconds. "102 on the left once you walk through the front double doors," read the message. Moments later I knocked on the door and to my surprise it was Chrissie, the girl from earlier by the cell phone store. She was dressed in a t-shirt and a pair of white panties, tightly fitted to her small frame. I stepped across the threshold and it was on from

there. Little did I know but this was a fatal mistake.

Chapter 9-Pretrial Confinement

One week later I was ultimately accused of sexually assaulting two women; Elena Gomez and Chrissie Moser. From the very first day of the allegations I was blackballed throughout my company. In the military a person accused of a crime is guilty before proven innocent, not the other way around. This was certainly true for me as I became known as the "Taylor-Boy" in my company while facing multiple charges. Any undesired task that came down the command pipe was assigned to yours truly. This was due to the fact that I couldn't do anything else. I was grounded from flight duty, restricted to base, and considered to be free labor if you ask me.

As dusk began to set in one shady afternoon, I received a phone call from Lieutenant Devon Boone. Boone was the unit's supply officer and seemed to be well respected around the company; from his peers down to the subordinates below. He spoke with an Italian accent, rapid and boisterous as he shouted through the line of my cell phone. "Hey Chief," he said while vocally resembling someone from the Italian mafia. "You's wanna lend me a hand," he asked. "I gotta get these mattresses swapped out for some new ones." I initially thought, "Here we go again with the abuse of power because I was in trouble."

My mind raced with endless excuses to use during the award moment of silence and then I remembered how much I actually enjoyed working with Lieutenant Boone. He was a pretty laid back guy and he had a way about himself that was different from the other "butter bars" in the unit. This was not to be expected considering the fact that he graduated from Harvard. I had actually worked with him before on this same type of work-detail so I had no problem helping him out. We were in route to the distribution center, but on the way he told me that he had to make a quick run by the warehouse.

Moments later we pulled into a lot of loose gravel and parked alongside the building. The front door of the warehouse was raised and there were a few Soldiers picking up supplies from the clerks. The operations were just like any other day in the warehouse. Lieutenant Boone went to speak with the officer in charge of the facility concerning some paperwork he needed. Meanwhile I waited in the main operation area of the warehouse for him to return. While standing there another Lieutenant by the name of Richardson approached me.

Lieutenant Richardson had recently arrived to Camp Humphreys just a few months prior, but he already appeared to be an influential person around the warehouse. He asked for a moment of my time to which I agreed. Richardson was a member of my church, but we rarely spoke other than Sunday mornings. "What could he want from me?" I thought as we came to a standstill. "What's up, I asked, what can I help you with?" Instantly his demeanor changed from the usual chipper person that he normally was to someone I didn't recognize at all. The corners of his mouth formed very sharp creases before he spoke and his eyebrows were mashed together in the middle of his forehead. "Listen up Chief," said Richardson; almost grinding his teeth as he spoke. "I'm coming to you man to man right now," he added with a stern point of his index finger. "Ok, I replied what is this about sir?" By this point my focus was on nothing else but him. He continued with the slightest inclination of slowing down as I listened to his rants. "Whenever there's a problem in my platoon I have to take care of it quickly; especially if it is affecting the work environment." "Sir what is this about?" I asked again. "You know my Soldier right?" "Who are you talking about?" I responded. "Specialist Marie Thomas," said Richardson." "Yes sir, I said, I know Thomas, she works here as a clerk I believe." "Well when you see her, said Richardson, don't speak to her, don't look, and avoid her by all means."

"Ok," I noted clearly confused about the entire conversation. I asked him once more in an attempt to get an answer, sir what is this about?" While displaying his true vaginal qualities as a so called "man" Richardson responded, "I'm not saying anything else chief, have your people gotten with you yet?" "What do you mean have my people gotten with me yet?" This time my temper was beginning to heat up because I thought he was joking, but his face portrayed a more serious image. I could see his demeanor getting more unstable and I knew for sure mine was doing the same. Luckily for both of us the conversation was interrupted with Lieutenant Boone walking up behind us.

"What's up Rich, Boone asked. "Oh…um nothing much, said Richardson as he smiled with an evil glare in my direction. "I better get back inside, you two stay out of trouble." He winked his eye at me as a reminder of our conversation. I guess Lieutenant Boone caught the tail end of the confrontation with Richardson because he stayed quiet until we got back in the truck. "Hey Taylor, what was that all about between you and Rich," he asked.

"Sir I'm really not sure yet, but I will get to the bottom of it." Boone being the laid back guy he was replied with a lackadaisical response and just as fast changed the subject. Man,

I wish I had his personality, just the attitude of appearing stress free all the time was amazing to me. Nothing could shake this guy at all; it was like he had ice water running through his blood. Once we got back to the company I was in for yet another surprise. I debated on whether I was going to bring the incident up to my commander or not. I thought to myself if I didn't bring it up then it would get back to her and that would make me seem like I was hiding something, especially considering the fact that my trial was less than thirty days away. On the other hand, if she was clueless, the spot light was on me again; doubled edge sword.

This was one of those moments I wish Ms. Cleo could have read my fortune just so I could know the outcome. Too bad for me, Ms. Cleo was locked up in jail somewhere for being a fraud. It took me a while, but I finally gave in. I walked extra slow towards Major Mitchell's office; thinking over and over again if this was the right thing to do. Little did I know, but the tables had already turned against me for the worse. I knocked on the door of her office and she told me to come in. To my surprise there were two other officers standing behind where I would soon be sitting. This was beyond normal, but I carelessly dismissed the observation. I popped a quick hand salute while snapping to the position of attention. "Ma'am CW2 Taylor reports," I said. "Have a seat, she replied while purposely avoiding eye contact. I took a deep breath and did as she asked. I attempted to speak, but mumbled due to nervousness.

Eventually I managed to tell her everything that happened at the warehouse. She paused for a moment and shuffled some papers on her desk into one neat pile. Finally, she refocused her attention towards me. "Well it appears that you are being investigated again, she said. Supposedly you have been texting and stalking a female down at the warehouse." There was an awkward silence that suddenly filled the room.

I shook my head while lowering it slightly towards my chest. "Ma'am I have full knowledge of this person who's making this accusation" I said, but before I could finish, she interrupted. She looked down at the documents on her desk and then back to me as she began to read. "Chief Taylor, I am placing you in pre-trial confinement." "You are suspected of violating the following articles of the Uniform Code of Military Justice," she added. I sat there and listened as she read off her list. "Charge one, Aggravated Sexual Assault, violation of Article 120. Charge two, "false official statement, violation of Article 107. Charge three, adultery, which is a violation of Article 134. She then went on to read off sixteen other charges, all of them carrying a maximum of up to five years per charge along with a mandatory sex offender registration just to add icing to the cake.

The rest of her reading was a blur. I heard nothing she said past charge three; adultery. I laughed a little to myself as I pondered on that charge alone. "Adultery, I thought, how convenient." Tammy surprised me with a birthday gift in the form of a divorce and now I was being charged with adultery; a common crime in the Army. The only difference between me and perhaps half of the rest of the military is... I got caught. There were rumors that even the commander herself was doing dirt behind her husband's back. The word on the street was her secret lover was the officer responsible for training other pilots in our company, so it was funny that she was charging me with adultery.

"Go ahead and stand up, said the commander, and place your hands behind your back." I did as I was told without putting up the slightest of a fight. I glared into her eyes as the two lieutenants placed the cold shackles around my wrist. A large lump began to form in my throat as I fought to hold back the tears "don't let them see you cry" I thought to myself. As the two officers tighten the cuffs, pinching my skin beneath the rigid iron restraints, a sudden blanket of comfort began to sooth me. I still can't explain the sense of calmness, but I was almost totally relaxed by the time they stuffed me in the back of an unmarked SUV. My position was no one else could accuse me of anything if I'm already locked up. I was less than thirty days away from trial and these people were doing their best to send me to

Leavenworth for something that I didn't do. Only time would

deliver the truth as the case unfolded.

Chapter 10-"Opening Statements"

After a year of being investigated and three days of fighting for a jury that would actually give a fair trial, the case began with the slam of the judge's gavel. I took a deep breath and quickly recalled the prior instructions from Tim in my head. "Emotionless, I thought to myself; be stiff as a board, and don't make eye contact with anyone on the jury." "Court is called to order, said the judge, Mr. Bailiff please call the members of the panel to the courtroom," she added.

"All Rise," yelled the bailiff as he snapped to the position of attention. The hinges on the door to the deliberation room squeaked loudly as he pulled it open. Five officers left from the pool of potential jurors marching in. They filed in one by one, all on the same step and at a moderate pace. I began to feel a pulse in my head as the last juror walked through the door. "Thump, thump, thump," echoed the sound of a drum in my head. The hairs on my neck began to rise as I felt the unwanted attention from a set of five eyes. I could feel each one of them glaring at me as they took their seats. "Please be seated," said the judge. "Court is called to order; all parties are again present to include the members of the jury. Ladies and gentlemen of the jury, in an earlier session the accused in the case plead not guilty to all specifications and charges. What will happen next is the opening statements from both the prosecution and the defense. I will advise you that these opening statements are not to be considered as evidence on your behalf. The statements are simply what each counsel thinks will be revealed as the trial progresses."

The judge pulsed behind the stand. You could hear, but not see the sound of papers being shuffled on the other side of her bench. Her long black robe revealed only the upper portion of her torso. A few more seconds elapsed as she continued to examine some documents. The clock behind her could be heard throughout the court room. Finally, she refocused her attention to the gallery and spoke.

"Government do you have an opening statement," asked the judge. The prosecutor stood up quickly from his table. "We do your honor." "You may proceed," the judge replied. The prosecutor gathered his notes and took his place behind the podium. He adjusted his tie while he cleared his throat. "Good morning Mr. President, he said. A successful predator is good at three things; identifying prey, knowing how to take full advantage and…." Before he could even get another word out, Tim was objecting to his previous statement. "Objection your honor, said Tim, improper propensity in an opening statement," he added.

"Captain Martin," said the judge. "As previously instructed I will forewarn you again that if your opening statement is going to go into any propensity evidence that is an improper statement; understood," she asked. "Yes your honor," replied the prosecutor. "The objection is sustained," said the judge, you may now continue." The prosecutor quickly re-gathered his thoughts and shifted the tone of his opening statement. "Panel members, for the next several days, the government will show that chief warrant officer Glenn Taylor was successful in plotting schemes so that he could get something he wanted in the end; his own sexual gratification."

The prosecutor shifted through his statement behind the podium smoothly as if he had practiced it several times. I could hear two stuck pages being separated by his fingers as he transitioned to the next portion of his script. "Now in this case, said the prosecutor, there is a lot of evidence. There are going to be several witnesses from both sides and a lot of information from all of them. After you hear all of the evidence along with the information from the witnesses, he said; you will see the accused for what he really did. You will see that the accused is someone who abused his power as an officer," said the prosecutor.

"We believe that the evidence will show he neglected the trust placed in him by three impressionable young girls. The government will also show that Glenn Taylor, an officer, got all

of these innocent young ladies in situations where he was in

control." I was burning with curiosity as to exactly how they

planned to prove this "control" theory of theirs. I turned slightly

to my right only to see Captain Daniels scribbling notes on his

yellow pad and Tim closely examining the rants from the

prosecutor. I took a sip of water from a cup sitting close to the

edge of our table. The water helped to sooth my parched pallet

as the prosecutor continued to deliver a crock of shit from a

bull's ass. "They were powerless, said the prosecutor; because of

this they were sexually assaulted. First the government will

show you how the accused picked out twenty-one year old Elena

Gomez. This is a Soldier that is new to the army. You will see

that Chief Taylor psychologically manipulated this young lady by

fraternizing with her through social media. This fraternization

will also be seen over the course of several months, said the

prosecutor, with the use of print out messages from the web.

Then you'll see how one day last October, he followed Elena out to a bar called All-stars.

Shortly after that he followed her into a bathroom and told her you're going to fuck me now bitch! As if this wasn't enough, he began to sexually assault her by grabbing the back of her head like a leash and forcing her to touch his penis. You'll hear how she finally convinced him that her friends were going to notice that she'd be gone a while and then he fled the scene immediately. He left her standing there alone, in that filthy bathroom with no regard for what he had just done.

After being questioned by CID agents, said the prosecutor; the government will show how the accused lied to them about where he had been that evening. The government will also show how later that same night the accused met another young impressionable Soldier on his way back to the gate in the ville; twenty year old Chrissie McNeil. You will see how they exchanged numbers, and with this girl that he had just met, he ended up going back to her room later on that night. Once inside of her room, you will see that the victim regained consciousness from her drunken state and vomited on her bed. She awoke after vomiting in her bed to a man naked beside her. "This man was someone she did not know, said the prosecutor; she had never seen this man before. She began to push him off and pleaded for him to stop." While being defined by the prosecutor as a "sexual predator" I could feel the eyes of the jurors as they seemed to have burned holes in my direction. "You will then see, said the prosecutor, how the accused became frustrated and tried to force private McNeil to have oral sex with him while she was lying in her own vomit. The accused finally gives up his attempt to have sex with McNeil and once again fleas the scene. He is later brought in by CID and yet again he lies about having sexual contact with McNeil. "Months earlier before these two instances took place, said the Prosecutor; he used his looks, charm, and his rank to befriend another Soldier who was also new to the Army. Nineteen-year old Marie Thomas had only been in the Army eight months when Chief Taylor met her." "He convinced her that it was ok for officers and junior enlisted Soldiers to hang out and spend time together. He lured her back to his room and once inside he had his way with her. Although she begged him to stop repeatedly, he continued to do with her as he wished, by pulling down her sweat pants, and her panties."

The prosecutor lowered his voice as he tried to connect with the members of the jury. "You will hear the witness tell you to your face, said the prosecutor, how it didn't matter that she said no. You will also hear how she basically describes herself as being treated like a piece of trash while Chief Taylor sexually assaulted her. Throughout all of these incidents you will also see that the accused was married. This will be voiced from his former wife, sergeant first class Tammy Hill," said the prosecutor. I still couldn't believe the reality was such; the government had flown Tammy in from Texas to Korea. It was the result of a statement she made against me months prior to the trial. Even with me basically begging Tammy's father for her to stay quiet, she did everything in her power to assist the government towards a conviction. The list of things she said against me was incredible, but I will never forget her telling law enforcement that she didn't believe I was capable of taking a girl in an alley and raping her, but she did believe that I would take advantage of a drunk female. If you were to ask me what's two plus two I would say four, the same as two times two. My point is you get the same result just a different way of stating it.

Marriages end every day all over the world. Some people look at it as being a sheet of paper with two joined names until one pisses on the other long enough to leave; others understand the true values of what it means to say "I do". Regardless of how a marriage comes to an end I'm sure many would agree that trying to impose harm on a once beloved is something only a demonic person would do.

"Finally, said the prosecutor, you will see that each one of these girls made very naïve decisions. They each placed themselves in situations that left them very vulnerable. The government would ask that you not focus on their naïve decisions but only on the actions of Chief Taylor. Thank you," he said as he flipped the yellow pages back to the beginning of his speech.

"Defense counsel said the judge, do you have an opening statement or do you wish to reserve?" "We do your honor" Tim replied. "You may proceed," the judged added. Tim stood up from behind our table; he used his right hand to fasten the middle buttons of his suit; and as if time waited on him, he took a sip of water from his glass that sat on the wooden table. I studied him as he leaned down toward Captain Daniels and whispered something in his ear. After an exchange of chit chat between the two of them, Tim finally approached the panel members. "Good Morning again," said Tim through a slightly distorted chuckle; "I believe this is the third time that I have said good morning to you all." I watched as all of the members of the jury smiled in response to Tim's joke. I had to firmly bite my lip to keep from smiling myself. "Chief Taylor did not sexually assault anyone," he continued, while stepping out from behind the wooden podium.

"The story here is much bigger than what the government has presented to you today. The evidence will show that the story is just like other things in life; they all have a back-story to them. The three of these young Soldiers also have a back- story that's different from what the government wants you to believe. The root of this story goes back to about a year ago," Tim said. "At that time, Chief Taylor was married through his eyes, to the love of his life. Now before all of this took place, his marriage had begun to unravel like most seem to nowadays in the military.

It's quite common for couples to be separated for up to years at a time in the Army as well as other branches of service" Tim expressed. "This is due to deployments, field training, and other exercises just to name a few. Like most marriages in the Army, Chief Taylor and his wife were separated from each other. She was being stationed on the other side of the world while Chief Taylor was here in Korea. This was the very thing that initiated the dark spiral of events in Chief's life. Chief did everything in his power to save his marriage. He did what he could but it what as they say, 'terminally broken.' That devastated Chief Taylor," Tim said. "At that time his wife was his heartbeat and after losing her he fell into a dark hole. Chief turned to alcohol in order to cope with his problems. Now I know this may not have been the best way to cope with his issues but it was what Chief Taylor turned to when his world was falling apart" Tim said.

Tim's voice grew louder in the courtroom after the ac switched off. "On the night of October 14th, which is one night out of these three instances that occurred," Tim added; the defense would ask that you please keep this night along with the other instances separate. This is due to the fact that they are significantly separate events. First I would like to talk about Elena Gomez".

"Before this alleged dirty bathroom scandal there was a relationship between the two. With Chief Taylor being in the dark place that he was emotionally, he befriended Gomez and contrary to what the government wants you to believe," Tim implied, "the witness was more than obliged to do the same. Although it was obviously inappropriate, the two of them began to share messages over social media. You'll see what she tried to hide from CID in those conversations. Thankfully we still have them and you'll be able to see the intimate and private things they BOTH talked about…not just Chief Taylor." Tim continued to paint the picture for the jurors for the next thirty minutes or so but before I knew it; it was time to call the first witness to the stand.

Chapter 11- "Show Time"

"Government you may now call the witness" said the judge. "Yes your honor," responded the prosecutor; his voice echoed with excitement throughout the courtroom. "The government calls Specialist Chrissie McNeil to the stand" he yelled. The roar of the crowd outside of the courtroom could be heard as McNeil walked through the double wooden doors. This was the first time I'd seen her since that night and everything about her about still appeared to be the same from the moment we met. She was very short, with pale skin, and the hairstyle that she wore was purposely cut to resemble a boy. She glared at me with her eyes, portraying a clear message of what was about to come. I paid no mind to her attempt to intimidate me and focused my attention to the front of the room.

"Please raise your right hand," said the prosecutor. "Do you swear or affirm that the testimony you are about to give today is the truth, the whole truth, and nothing but the truth, so help you God?" "I do," said McNeil. The prosecutor lowered his hand and motioned Chrissie towards the witness stand. She

walked up the two small steps that led to a leather finished chair

behind a microphone. "Good Afternoon" said the prosecutor

with a fake smile bright enough to light up New York City.

"Can you please state your name for the record" he asked.

"Specialist Chrissie McNeil" she replied. "Specialist McNeil if

you would take a few moments to tell us a little bit about

yourself." Chrissie cleared her throat just like a man would;

using two hands to adjust her collar around her neck for comfort.

She even tried to speak like a man as she started with her small

military background.

"I am specialist Chrissie A. McNeil she said. I am

assigned to the 235th Military Intelligence Battalion here at Camp

Humphreys. This is my first duty station she added, and I've

been here about two years so far." "Thank you Specialist said the

prosecutor." "Now I know it may be difficult" he said while

shifting the tone of his questioning, but can you tell me what you remember happening on the night of Oct 14th 2011?" he asked. Chrissie leaned in towards the microphone and answered; "I only remember some of the night because I was drinking." "That's ok the prosecutor insisted, "Tell us what you do remember."

Chrissie exhaled from a deep breath and stuttered until finally gathering her words. "I was twenty years old at the time and knew that I would get in trouble if I got caught drinking" she said. "We all started drinking in my room but decided to go out to the ville." The prosecutor walked from behind the podium and casually strolled to the witness stand. In his hands he carried a box of drinking glasses and a computer generated photo that was used as evidence in the case. Everyone in the courtroom watched as he stooped over to place the wooden box on the floor.

"Can you please tell the panel members what is this photo of" he asked. Without even looking at the picture Chrissie replied. "This is one of the drinking glasses that I drank from that night" she insisted. "I had three Vodka Red Bulls in a glass just like that" she added; clearly a rehearsed answer. Just to add a bit of flare to her story, Chrissie continued to express her night of wild alcoholic suppressions; naming drink, after drink, after drink.

"I had a White Russian after the Vodka Red Bull, it was in a glass that exact size and then I downed a Jager bomb." "Damn I thought to myself, this bitch must have been thirsty." Only a man could put away drinks like that but then I remembered she was trying to play on the theory of being gay. Months earlier during an interview with CID, she stated she had no idea how a man ended up in her room; more than that beside her in bed. This was significant especially considering the fact that she was a so called "lesbian."

The only question that was left unanswered in her story was about the DNA. The DNA collected as evidence revealed the traces of two men; yours truly and another man who was never identified till this day. Only time would reveal the truth of Chrissie McNeil. I listened to every word as she continued with her story. After carefully painting the picture about her level of drunkenness, the prosecutor changed his line of questioning. "What do you remember happening later that night" he asked. I watched as Chrissie's entire demeanor changed from stern to somber almost instantly.

"I remember waking up in my room because I was vomiting heavily" she said. "The next thing I remember was a guy in bed beside me. I didn't get a good look at his face but I do remember that he was black" she added. "Can you tell us whether he was dressed or not" the prosecutor asked. "We both were naked Chrissie replied; almost faster than a well-rehearsed skit. "How do you know he was naked he asked. "Because I could see his penis" she said.

Before the prosecutor could ask his next question someone's cell phone went off behind us in the gallery. "You are excused!" said the judge, quickly reprimanding the spectator as he left the courtroom. "Again I will remind everyone to silence their phones," the judge instructed. "Government you may continue she said. "Thank you your honor." "Specialist

McNeil, please continue" said the prosecutor. "I remember the man making kissing and sucking noises in my ear. He tried to roll on top of me and put his penis inside of me" she added. "When you say inside of you are you referring to your vagina" the prosecutor suggested.

"Yes exactly" said Chrissie, quickly answering the loaded question. "How do you know he was trying to put his penis inside of your vagina" the prosecutor asked. Chrissie lowered her head and paused then she looked back up at the prosecutor and suddenly began to cry. "It's ok he said, I can only imagine how hard this may be." I looked at her as she reached for a tissue from a box on the edge of the witness stand. Her eyes started to turn red as time passed. She snatched another tissue from the small white box and finally started to speak. Her voice could be heard but only muffled as she cried her response through a single sheet of Kleenex. "I know it was his penis she finally uttered; because the only other time I've felt that pain was when I lost my virginity". Her tears seemed real and sincere to me but left the slightest impression with my defense team. Tim scribbled down a quick note and slid it to me as Chrissie continued her award winning performance. I glanced down towards the yellow note pad only to see the words "crocodile tears" scribbled along the top edge. Definitely words of comfort considering the mood her tears caused throughout the courtroom.

"When did he finally leave you alone?" the prosecutor asked. "Once I called my friend she said, that's when he finally got dressed and left." After an hour or so had past, he finally ended his questioning. "Nothing further your honor said the prosecutor. "Defense council would you like to cross" asked the judge. "Yes your honor Tim replied, but the defense would first like to request a brief recess for a comfort break." "Very well said the judge, court is in recess until 13:30."

Small chatter swarmed the room until the last soul crossed the threshold of the door. The clock on the wall ticked a steady rhythm which echoed as I sat there alone. All I could think about was going home, packing up my gear, and starting a new life. Only time would tell if such freedom would be within my reach. I lowered my head towards the faded blue carpet of the courtroom floor; my eyes were planted in a downward gaze. At that very moment I only wished for comfort as tears started to form on the edge of each lid.

Suddenly the door of the gallery opened and in walked Tim and Jack followed by other spectators there for the show. The prosecutors barged in with a team of Soldiers who carried additional boxes, which I assumed were for the case considering the red tape across the front. I watched as the crowd of spectators scuffled to find their seats. It was crazy to see some of these people. There were people from all over in the gallery of the courtroom; most of which I didn't know. Even guys from my unit showed up and sat on the front row, Major Mitchell included. I didn't know how to feel about her being there considering the circumstances. I understood that she had a job to do as my commander but I had felt a little uneasy about her ever since my pretrial lock up, especially considering the fact that I was released only seven days later.

"You ok Glenn" Tim Whispered who was sitting on the other side of Jack. "Why is she here" I asked relaying my discomfort with Mitchell's presence. "Don't worry about her" said Tim. "It's an open courtroom so anyone can come in and sit. Besides" he added; wouldn't you like to see her face when you're fully acquitted of this garbage?" I cracked a slight smile in an attempt to be at ease. A few moments passed before the judge reentered the room. "All rise!" yelled the bailiff who stood by the door of the deliberation room. "Please be seated" said the Judge.

"Court is hereby called to order. Bailiff if you would please call the members of the panel" The bailiff reached for the handle of the door and yelled yet again "All rise!" he shouted, even louder than before. The jury marched in and casually took their seats. "Government please call the witness," said the judge. "Yes your honor," said the prosecutor while signaling one of his Soldiers standing by the gallery door. The young

161

Sergeant left the courtroom and moments later returned with Chrissie. She walked swifter this time almost in a hurry. The prosecutor reminded Chrissie she was under oath as round two began.

"Defense Counsel you may begin" said the judge. "Yes your honor" Tim replied. "Specialist McNeil good morning" Tim said, loud enough for his voice to fill the courtroom. "Good morning Sir" she replied. "It's fair to say that you've experienced memory loss during the night you believe you were sexually assaulted correct." "Correct Sir." "But that's not the first time you've experienced a blackout correct; just to clear up the definition of a black out, it is when you remember certain things from the night before then there's a break in your memory and then it kind of picks back up again" Tim asked. "Yes that is correct" Chrissie agreed.

"So you've had these blackouts before and on the night that you believed you were sexually assaulted you had one of these blackouts; is that correct?" "Yes sir" she said with a slight

162

hesitation in her voice. "Isn't it true for you" Tim added, "that

alcohol is a contributing factor to these blackouts?" Chrissie

answered but seemed offended at the questioning from Tim.

"Yes" Chrissie said, suddenly changing to a less lucid tone. "So

it's important in this case to understand how much you had to

drink that night correct" Tim asked. "That is also correct" she

replied with a touch of sass in her response. Question for

question Tim sought after answers; uncovering every inch of the

devious plots of the prosecution. Within the first hour of his

cross examination Tim had wiped several pieces of Chrissie's

bullshit story from the surface of the truth. She confessed to

being coached by the prosecutors, agreed that they schemed

together days before the trial and overall contradicted other

portions of her statement; severely damaging her credibility.

After his questioning had ended the judge allowed the prosecutor

to redirect. Between their table and ours, the arguments went

back and forth like a tennis match.

Soon the shots from both sides ceased to fire. Chrissie

was finally released but just as fast, it was time for Elena to take the stand. Just as he did with Chrissie the prosecutor swore Elena to the truth. The prosecutor started with his line of questioning just as before; allowing Elena to provide details on her background before beginning his direct examination. Elena stated that she was hanging out with some friends drinking in her room. She later claimed that they went to the ville in search of a night club. Throughout the majority of her testimony I only remember thinking of how it sounded so familiar compared to McNeil's. It was almost like they were coached to say the exact same thing. Regardless of the scheme organized by the government to put me in prison, Tim delivered justice in my name.

Every dollar I had invested with Tim was paying off. With each witness that took the stand, he delivered a formal can of ass thrashing that dismantled the alleged rape allegations blow for blow. Elena confessed to her lies and even perjured herself during her testimony. She said that "it was all fun and games" to do what she did. Adding injury to insult, she was called out in the middle of her testimony for smirking during questions from Tim. I think that was enough to convince the jury in my favor. I had spent a year of my life being investigated for what she considered to be "fun and games" now she was laughing about it on the witness stand. This in itself was not the most bizarre twist of this story however. The straw that broke the camel's back would have to be the testimony of my dear "Sweet Marie." This was the most unique story of them all.

When asked how was it possible that she had an *orgasm* while supposedly being raped by me, Marie said that her body betrayed her and that she couldn't control herself. I'm sure many women would agree that it would be virtually impossible to have an orgasm with someone violently raping them. After six days of a trial and seven hours of deliberating, the jury finally returned with a verdict for my fate. I will never forget the sound of the judge's voice as she asked that infamous question; "Has the jury reached a verdict" she asked. "Yes your" honor said the president of the jury. "CW2 Glenn Taylor Please rise" said the Judge. The three of us stood up at the same time, me, Jack and Tim. "Please announce the verdict said the judge." My legs felt as if they were going to give out from underneath me as he read. "In regards to Charge one we find CW2 Glenn Taylor Not Guilty, Charge two Not Guilty, Charge three Not Guilty. The president of the jury read off not guilty verdicts for each charge with the exception of two; adultery because I was still "married" at the time and fraternization due to my rank. At that very moment I could have cared less. The case was finally over!

Chapter 12-"Karma"

A few weeks after the trial the smoke had cleared and the gossip of my outcome was the only thing still lingering around the company? Operation serial rapist was the topic of discussion around the Unit and to be honest, I could give two shits about the rumors. I even found a bit of humor out of the things that I learned from other people about myself. It's amazing in the Army how far stories can be stretched from the truth.

During one of my last days left in Korea I received a call from my mother-in- law Mrs. Hill. It wasn't out of the norm for her to call me but I could sense something was wrong from the tone of her voice. "Glenn I need to tell you something she said, but I need you to be strong when you hear it." "Yes ma'am" I replied, baffled by her hesitation and eager to hear what it was she had to say. There was a brief moment of silence on the phone. "Glenn are you sitting down?" she asked. Whenever someone asks if I'm sitting down bad news usually follows.

"I take my coffee standing up, so what's this about?" I asked.

"Well you know we've been having some terrible snow storms here in Alabama over the past few weeks or so." "Yes ma'am" I said. "I've seen the footage on the news" I added. "Well I won't waste any more of your time" said Mrs. Hill. Tammy was on her way to work this morning and she was involved in an accident." "Oh no is she ok?" I asked. I expressed a bit of concern in an attempt to hide my careless attitude, to be honest at this point in my life I could have cared less about anything that happened to her. She could've died a slow burning death and I doubt I would have pissed on her if she was on fire!

My thoughts would soon come back to haunt me. Mrs. Hill paused for a minute and then she finally revealed the suspenseful news. "Glenn she lost control of her car! She was speeding to get to work and ran into the back of a fuel truck." "Oh my God is she ok?" I asked. "She's in very critical condition" said Mrs. Hill. The truck exploded killing the driver on the spot. Tammy's car caught on fire as well but she was pulled out before it could explode. She's on life support now and the doctors are saying that her chances of survival are very slim."

I wanted to say something but couldn't. It was like my words were trapped inside my mouth. After everything Tammy did I had actually wished for a day like this to happen to her. Now that it had really taken place I couldn't help but wonder if I should have felt guilty. All I could remember was the fact that she asked for a divorce on my birthday and I was still in the dark as to why. Not only that but she lied to my commander and most of all to CID in a truly vindictive manner.

"Glenn, Tammy is in a coma" Mrs. Hill added. "The doctors have given up on her chances of waking up ever again. I know you and her are not on the best of terms" she said "but I wanted to ask you something as her mother. I was wondering if you would come to Alabama to help me with her. I can't get around like I used to due to my condition and I could really use your help with her." This was perhaps one of the most challenging questions I've ever had to answer in my life, but after a while I said "Sure I'll be there in a few days." "Thank you; this really means a lot to me" Mrs. Hill replied.

"There's just one more thing I need to ask you" she said just before hanging up the phone. "What's that?" I asked. "The doctors don't expect her to make a recovery at all and as I told you earlier she's on life support. They have given up hope for her and they need someone to make a decision about her being taken off." "Ok" I said" "What does that have to do with me?" "Everything" replied Mrs. Hill. You are still her legal husband according to the state of Alabama even though the divorce is pending. You are the only person who can make the decision on whether she's taken off life support or not. I'm hoping and praying that you can find it in your heart to do the right thing." "Do the right thing?" I thought as Mrs. Hill and I finally said our goodbyes on the phone. Later on that night I booked a flight and arrived at the hospital a few days later. When I got there I was met by my mother and father in law who were both pretty upset as expected. "It's good to see you" said Mr. Hill. The three of us shared a hug before I was finally led to the room where they were keeping Tammy. The nurse hesitated at the door before letting me in.

"Sir I must warn you said the nurse; she suffered a very blunt impact from the driver's side window and the swelling hasn't gone down yet. You probably won't be able to recognize her because of third degree burns that cover about eighty percent of her body. Just brace yourself" the nurse insisted. I slowly cracked the door and walked in the room. The sound of the EKG played with a steady rhythm of Tammy's heartbeat. The room was dimmed with the exception of an overhead light that shined down on her bed. I stood there for a moment watching as she laid there hooked up to multiple wires.

She appeared to be lifeless as the sight of her face depicted a horrific tragedy. Her body was wrapped in white gauze from her head to her feet and the smell of death clouded the room. This smell was like no other scent I've smelled before in my life. "I'll leave you two so you can have some privacy" said the nurse. Lost for words I took a seat in the small blue chair near her bedside. I couldn't believe that she was here, lying there in a vegetative state. I studied the area where her face normally was. The bandages only revealed her eyes which were slightly open but motionless as if she was in fact dead already.

I began to replay our friendship from the military, long talks on the phone, and then ultimately our short lived marriage. For a moment I remembered the good times we shared together and wished they had never ended. Then I quickly thought about the fact that this was the same woman who did everything in her power to hurt me, including helping detectives to form a case against me. I was facing years in prison, years in the double digits to be exact. Just to know that she was involved played over and over again in my mind. I thought about the nasty emails she wrote, the lies she told, and more than anything the words "I want a divorce"; not to mention the fact that it was on my birthday serving as a constant reminder. Just as I was re-living the pain and agony she caused in my life, Tammy's doctor entered the room. "Mr. Taylor" he said as the door closed quickly behind him. "My name is Doctor Benjamin Morton; I'm your wife's primary care provider." I quickly corrected him, "she's my current spouse sir but not at all my wife." "I apologize said the doctor. I'm here to give you an update about Tammy's condition as I was told you just arrived. As you may already know she suffered several injuries, some more serious than others. Upon impact her head collided with the driver's side window, she sustained eight broken ribs, and her legs were crushed from her hips down to her ankles."

"Believe it or not those are the minor injuries" the doctor continued. Some of the more serious injuries include a cerebral hematoma, paralysis, and as you can see third degree burns cover the majority of her body" he added. "Dr. Morton any idea how this all happened?" I asked. "There is an officer in the south wing of the ICU working on another case right now, said the doctor but he is also aware that you are here. He will be able to provide you with more details as to what actually happened. He was in fact on duty at the time and the video footage from his patrol car captured the entire accident."

I later had the chance to sit down with the patrolman and from the moment I saw his face I clearly remembered where I'd seen him before. His pot belly and the southern accent was one that I could never forget. It was Officer Ivan B. Stone; the same dick that basically tricked me into the psychiatric ward on my birthday. He obviously had no recollection of who I was. It was to be expected considering the amount of people he probably came in contact with on a daily basis. "Officer Stone this is Glenn Taylor, said Doctor Morton. He's the spouse of the lady in room 107."

The Officer extended his hand and I met it with a firm grip to which I purposely tried to crush. "Wow that's quite a grip ya got there son" said Stone with a look of concern on his face. "Sorry sir, I must not know my own strength." Getting straight into the conversation I changed the subject to what we were there for. "Sir I understand that you were actually on duty the day of Tammy's accident." "Yes the weather was really bad and I had already responded to about two accidents prior to hers" said Officer Stone. I was the first responder on site for her as well" he added. I listened carefully to him as he held on to his round brown police hat in a regretful posture.

"How close were you exactly?" I asked. "Sir I think it would be best if I show you so you can see for yourself" he insisted. He used a remote control that was on the table we were sitting at and turned on the TV that was mounted to the wall. The quality of the video was fuzzy for a few seconds, there were squawks of radio traffic being heard and then out of the blue the picture cleared. The first thing I saw was heavy snow falling on a slightly congested highway. That image was soon followed by a guy on a motor cycle. "He must be insane" I thought to myself. "There's no way I would be on a bike in that weather." He passed and was soon trailed by a fuel a truck. I could feel my heart beginning to beat faster as I recalled the details about the accident. The next vehicle that came into the picture was one I had seen before, it was Tammy's black Maxima. I instantly recognized the car because of her custom made tags that abbreviate the words "honey bun." My eyes were locked on the TV screen. I'd heard about everything that happened, seen the aftermath but I still wanted to see it for myself.

Just as the story was told I watched as her car suddenly lost control, flipped three or four times, and then slammed into the back of the truck. I could see her being tossed around the inside just before the two vehicles collided. The explosion was like something out of a movie. I couldn't believe what I was seeing. I watched as Officer Stone darted towards the crash in his patrol car. He could be seen in the video assisting another gentleman and together they dragged her out of the wreckage.

"Sir I've seen enough I said; you can turn it off now." I really didn't know how to feel, the sense of feeling anything at all had been damaged due to my shortcomings. For the last year I wanted anything bad that could happen to happen to her and no one else but her to be exact. I pondered yet again the torrent of emotions and how I should have felt especially now considering the tables had ironically turned. The time was 12:31 a.m. January 23rd and you would never guess what day it was, Tammy's birthday of all days.

I snapped out of my daydream to the sound of the officer's voice "Mr. Taylor said Officer Stone, we are in the process of conducting a full investigation. We are trying to find out exactly what took place before, during, and after Tammy's accident. So far the only thing that we've been able to discover is the fact that she was on the phone while she was driving and perhaps texting as well." "Here are the messages" said Stone. "As you can see the time/date stamp match the phone records to someone named Mike Clitoriley. Does that name ring a bell to you?" he asked. "Yes that's her commander" I replied with a shocking look on my face. "I'm quite familiar with him. He went above and beyond to keep me from contacting Tammy while I was in Korea. He wrote my commander stating that I was harassing her and it was affecting her work performance."

"It's such a small world" I thought to myself. It's kind of funny how life plays out. I smiled a little as I read over the messages between Tammy and Clitoriley. All the answers that I had been in search of were now in front of my face, literally. I read messages that were dated back to just a few weeks after we were married. Some of them were rated PG., but most of them revealed Tammy's true colors.

"Just left the unit, I'm gonna grab a bottle of wine and then I'm headed your way."- Big Mike

"Hurry up, cuz I'm starting to wet up those black panties you like so much."- Tammy

I read over the messages carefully, examining each of them for more answers. Some of them I couldn't believe. At this very moment it made sense as to why she was late picking me up from the airport during my R&R; More than likely she was busy being spanked down by "Big Mike" as my flight landed. I couldn't continue to focus on speculation or wonder why she did the things she did; I had a decision to make. Officer Stone advised me of the department's intentions throughout the rest of their investigation. I agreed to keep my phone close by in case I was needed for anything else.

"Knock, Knock" said a voice through the banging of knuckles on the other side of the door. "Excuse me Mr. Taylor" said Doctor Morton while peeking his head in through the crack of the door. "May I have one more word with you?" he asked. "Sure, you mind giving us a moment Officer Stone?" I asked as nicely as I could but it was certainly a false gesture of politeness as I still remember our highway encounter. "Most certainly" said Stone. He gathered his documents and re-tucked his shirt tail before finally leaving the room.

"Mr. Taylor" said Morton. There is no easy way to say

this so I'm just going to say it. I've already informed the Hill family that we have given up all hope on Tammy ever waking up again; there's nothing else we can do. It would be best if we brought closure to her suffering" said Doctor Morton. He was most certainly right, I needed to end her suffering. "Can I have a little more time with her?" I asked. "Sure, said Doctor Morton. Take your time sir."

I started walking back to Tammy's room and the EKG could be heard through the depths of the door as I turned the last corner. I paused with the knob of the door in my hand and thought quickly again about Tammy's condition before walking in. The lights above had been dimmed by the nurse. I sat and read over the letter of consent, the piece of paper that would terminate her life being supported by this little machine. "You did a number on me" I whispered as if she could hear, while fighting back a dangling tear. Happy Birthday you said and you asked for a divorce, now I'm going to pull this plug with no remorse. Before I knew it the room was quiet, Tammy was dying and I didn't mind it. I stood there and watched as the monitor beeped one last time, marking the end of her life as the machine flat lined. Spiteful and vindictive my actions may seem, but the next morning I woke up to my alarm because it was ALL just a dream!

THE END

Made in the USA
Charleston, SC
10 May 2016